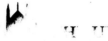

MOTHER GOOSE

MOTHER GOOSE

A Pantomime

by Chris Denys and Chris Harris

JOSEF WEINBERGER PLAYS

LONDON

MOTHER GOOSE
First published in 2001
by Josef Weinberger Ltd
12-14 Mortimer Street, London, W1T 3JJ

ISBN 0 85676 256 3

Name of Licensee
Play Title
Place of Performance
Dates and Number of Performances
Audience Capacity
Ticket Prices

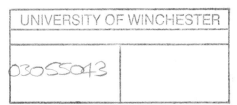

Printed by Watkiss Studios Ltd, Biggleswade, Beds.

This Pantomime of **MOTHER GOOSE** was first produced by the Bristol Old Vic Company at the Theatre Royal, Bristol on December 3rd 1993 with the following cast:

MEPHISTO, *the Malevolent*	Mark Buffery
FAIRY GOOSEFEATHER	Heather Williams
SILLY BILLY	Patrick Miller
JACK	Louise Plowright
JILL	Lisa Bowerman
SQUIRE GOODWORTHY	David Glover
MOTHER GOOSE	Chris Harris
PRISCILLA	Aubrey Budd
KING GANDER	David Glover
VILLAGERS, FOOTMAN, PARLOURMAIDS, WATER NYMPHS, WITCHES, GOSLINGS	The Dancers of ACRODANCE 2000

Directed by Chris Denys
Designed by Geoffrey Scott
Music Directed by John O'Hara
Music Supervised by Neil Rhoden
Choreography by Gail Gordon
Lighting Designed by Tim Streader
Sound Designed by Mark Gallagher

Characters

MEPHISTO THE MALEVOLENT	An evil magician
FAIRY GOOSEFEATHER	Patron Fairy of Goslings and Geese
SILLY BILLY	Mother Goose's Mill Hand
JACK	The Hero
JILL GOODBODY	The Heroine
SQUIRE GOODBODY	Her Father
MOTHER GOOSE	A poor widow woman
PRISCILLA	Her Goose

CHORUSES OF: VILLAGERS, FOOTMEN and PARLOURMAIDS, WATER NYMPHS, WITCHES, GOSLINGS

Scenes

ACT ONE

Scene 1:   PROLOGUE (*In front of Panto Gauze*)

Scene 2:   THE VILLAGE GREEN – OUTSIDE MOTHER
                GOOSE'S WINDMILL AND COTTAGE

Scene 3:   THE INTERIOR OF MOTHER GOOSE'S COTTAGE

Scene 4:   LOVER'S LANE (*Front Cloth*)

Scene 5:   MOTHER GOOSE'S PALACE OF GOLD (*Front Cloth*)

Scene 6:   THE EDGE OF THE FOREST (*Gauze*)

Scene 7:   THE WATERFALL OF YOUTH AND BEAUTY

ACT TWO

Scene 1:   BEFORE PANTO GAUZE

Scene 2:   THE VILLAGE GREEN (*As Act One, Scene Two*)

Scene 3:   THE EDGE OF THE FOREST (*Gauze, as Act One, Scene Six*)

Scene 4:   A CLEARING IN THE FOREST

Scene 5:   THE EDGE OF THE FOREST (*Gauze, as Act One, Scene Six*)

Scene 6:   A CLEARING IN THE FOREST (*As Act Two, Scene Four*)

Transformation to:

Scene 7:   THE PALACE OF KING GANDER

Scene 8:   LOVER'S LANE (*Front Cloth, as Act One, Scene Four*)

Scene 9:   (*Walkdown and* FINALE)

AUTHORS' NOTE

This Pantomime is intended to be "traditional" in that the Principal Boy is a girl, the Dame is a man, the story is told clearly with as much action and knock-about as possible and, very importantly, it is local to the town or city in which it is performed. It's also meant to be great fun – both for the audience and for those who perform and present it.

The local references in this script relate to Bristol – where it was first produced in 1993 and again in 1998 before transferring to Cheltenham in 1999 (where it acquired references to Lansdown, Little Herberts and Up Hatherly) so please feel free to localise as necessary and desirable.

Also, the staging is as described because we were working in beautifully equipped theatres with excellent design and production departments able to give us anything we asked for. It doesn't have to be like that, of course, and can be adapted to how much – or how little – you have at your disposal.

The stage directions, groundplans and indicated lighting, sound, follow spot and pyrotechnic cues are only intended as suggestions and not to be in any way prescriptive or cause pain.

The only sort of "flash" units allowed by Fire Officers these days are ruinously expensive and we always wrote our scripts with a liberal use of these effects only to cut them back when we saw what it was going to cost.

Of course, the Goose is a very important costume/prop because she really must look utterly loveable or else nobody will care much what happens to her. Her honks are best made by a Duck Caller – which can be got from anybody who shoots ducks – or from a shop which supplies them.

The Music:
Pantomime audiences do like to know the tunes so we have always used either current and perennial favourites as written or taken well-known melodies and written lyrics which stand as part of the plot and move the story along.

Some of the music we have used is out of copyright (eg, the Act One Finale is set to a well-known piece of Wagner and is clear) *but other melodies are still in copyright and you will need to pay for these if you use them through the Performing Rights Society* (who offer a special – and very reasonable – deal for Pantomimes).

Mostly, though, we have found that producers prefer to choose their own music to suit and show off the particular voices of their cast.

ACT ONE

Scene One

In front of Pantomime Gauze. A Flash DL. (**Pyro Q.1; SQ.1; LXQ.1; FSQ.1**) *MEPHISTO appears, sees the AUDIENCE and recoils in disgust.*

MEPHISTO: Ah! What a fright!
               What a gruesome sight!
               What a hideously happy crew!
               But I'll wipe all traces
               Of smiles from your faces.
               Yes – I've a surprise for you.
               Oh, you may hiss!
               And you may boo!

               (*They do!*)

               But I tell you this –
               Before I'm through –
               Your scorn will be irrelevant.
               You'll come to naught,
               If you try to thwart –
               Mephisto, the Malevolent!
               I'll spoil the joy
               Of girl and boy.
               There'll be no church bells' chime.
               The goodies will perish
               And I will flourish
               By the end of this pantomime.
               Well . . . it's only fair
               That I have my share
               Of glory like I oughter.
               I'll beat them all
               By the curtain call
               And marry the Squire's daughter.

               (*A Flash DR.* (**Pyro Q.2; LXQ.2; FSQ.2**) *FAIRY
               GOOSEFEATHER appears.*)

FAIRY: Oh no you won't.

MEPHISTO: Oh yes I will.

FAIRY: Oh no you won't, fowl feathered fiend. Leave these jolly
               good types alone.

Flit awf to your cave,
You fearful knave.
This is a demonless zone.
(*To the AUDIENCE.*) What ho! Golly!
I say – how jolly –
All you kiddies and Dads and Mums –
Just stick together
With Fairy Goosefeather.
We'll be the most spiffing chums.

MEPHISTO: Oh, go and look after Cinderella –
Dick Whittington or some other fella.
Leave Mother Goose to me.

FAIRY: Mother Goose?

MEPHISTO: Yes, Mother Goose. I find she's at the bottom
Of all this felicity
Infecting the City.
They're even good in Cotham.
She gets on my wick.
She cares for the sick.
She's a bigger blight than BUPA.
She's good – she's nice –
She's devoid of vice . . .

FAIRY: She's absolutely super!

MEPHISTO: But I will lead
Her into greed.
I'll snare her with my tether.
For good or ill,
She will do my will
By the power of – the Black Feather!

(*A very dramatic chord.*)

FAIRY: (*Appalled*) The Black Feather?

MEPHISTO: Ha-haar!

FAIRY: You go too fa-haar.
I never was aghaster!

MEPHISTO: No time to waste
For I'm in haste
To bring her to disaster.
Mephisto's the name

And evil's the game.
There's not a hotter plotter.
I'll foil all of you
But, for now, adieu.

(*Flash.* (**PyroQ.3; SQ.2; LXQ.3; FSQ.1A**) *He disappears DL.*)

FAIRY: Well! What a beastly rotter!
But don't fret, my dears.
Forget your fears.
Fairy Goosefeather's wise and wary.
I've always a spell
To make all well.
I'm a very good class of fairy.
So just keep calm
While I find a charm
To erase him from the scene
And I'll introduce-you
To the lasses and youths-who
Are dancing . . . on Redland Green!

(*Dissolve through gauze* (**LXQ.4**) *to:*)

Scene Two

Village Green. MOTHER GOOSE'S windmill. The Gauze Flies Out. (**Fly Q.1; LXQ. 5; FSQ.2A**)

Song: **WHEN THE SUN SAYS "GOOD MORNING"** (*BILLY* (*Wearing Policeman's helmet and cape over costume*) *and VILLAGERS*)

WHEN THE SUN SAYS "GOOD MORNING" TO YOU,
SHOUT ALOUD "GLAD TO MEET YOU, HOW D'YOU DO?"
SMILE YOUR CARES AWAY DOWN SUNNYSIDE LANE,
ANKLE DEEP IN BLOSSOMS AGAIN.
JOIN THE BIRDS IN THEIR SUNRISE PARADE,
LET YOUR HEART SING A HAPPY DAWN SERENADE.
WITH THE NIGHT BEHIND,
YOU'LL AWAKE AND FIND
THERE'S A WORLD FULL OF RAINBOWS IN VIEW
WHEN THE SUN SAYS "GOOD MORNING" TO YOU.

(*JACK enters UL.*)

JACK: Hello, everybody . . .

BILLY: Jack.

JACK: Hello, Billy. Isn't it a wonderful day?

BILLY: That isn't what you've been saying this past two weeks . . . You've been a regular old glumboots.

JACK: Only because Jill was away. But today she's coming home and I'm . . . bursting with joy.

(*FSQ.3*)

JACK: (*Sings:*) WITH THE ONE I LOVE FAR AWAY,
                  I'VE BEEN PINING:
LOST AND SAD AND MISERABLE ALL DAY LONG.
BUT TODAY SHE RETURNS AND THE SUN IS SHINING;
SKIES ARE BLUE AND YOU'LL HEAR ME SINGING THIS
                  SONG:

(*FSQ.3A; LXQ.6*)

(*JACK, BILLY and the VILLAGERS repeat the chorus.*)

BILLY: Here she comes now . . .

JACK: Quick, everybody . . . Hide!

(*They all hide as JILL enters from UL.*)

JILL: Hello, every . . . Why there's nobody here . . . (*FSQ.3B*)
(*Sings:*) HOME AT LAST BUT NOBODY HERE TO MEET
                        ME.
ALL MY FRIENDS HAVE VANISHED INTO THIN AIR.
I HOPED THAT THEY'D ALL BE RUNNING TO GREET ME.
DID THEY FORGET? OR ARE THEY HIDING SOMEWHERE?

ALL: (*Leaping out*) HERE!

(*FSQ.3C; LXQ.7*)

(*JACK, JILL, BILLY and the VILLAGERS repeat the chorus to the end.*)

(*FSQ.3D*)

JACK: Oh, Jill . . .

JILL:	Oh, Jack . . .
BILLY:	I'm here . . .
JILL:	Oh, Jack . . .
JACK:	Oh, Jill . . . I know you've only been away a week but it's been like a lifetime to me . . .
JILL:	And to me. Oh, Jack . . .
JACK:	Oh, Jill . . .
JILL:	Oh, Jack . . .
BILLY:	SQUEAKS.
BOTH:	Oh BILLY!
JILL:	But, Billy, why are you dressed like that?
BILLY:	(*Proudly*) It's my uniform. I've got a new job. I'm the Community Constable and Bailiff of the Borough. I keep the peace, pick up the pieces, catch the criminals and collect the debts. Oh, and I'm responsible for all the rabbits.
JILL:	The rabbits?
BILLY:	Yeh. I'm the burrow surveyor.
	(*All laugh – no groans, all should be enthusiastic to BILLY'S gags.*)
JILL:	But collecting debts must be a very unfriendly job.
BILLY:	Oh no. People are always asking me to call again.
JILL:	Don't you get a lot of doors slammed in your face?
JACK:	No, his face has always looked like that.
	(*All Laugh.*)
BILLY:	You may laugh . . . (*To the AUDIENCE.*) And you *may* laugh . . . but I arrested a burglar in the butchers only this morning.
JILL:	A burglar in the butchers? What was he doing?

BILLY: Chop lifting.

JILL: Oh Jack . . .

JACK: Oh Jill . . .

BILLY: Oh blimey . . .

           (*Music: intro.*) (***FSQ.4; LXQ.8***)

           ***Song:* ONE HOUR OF LOVE** (*JACK and JILL Duet.*)

JACK: I'D GIVE THE SUNSHINE TO GAZE IN YOUR EYES.

JILL: I'D GIVE THE STARS FROM THE BRIGHTEST OF SKIES.

BOTH: I'D GIVE THE SONG OF THE BIRDS ON THE TREE
           FOR THAT, TO ME,
           IS LOVE'S MELODY.
           I'D GIVE THE FLOWERS FROM THE FAIREST OF BOWERS
           I'D GIVE THE GREAT SKY OF BLUE
           I'D GIVE THE JOYS OF THE WHOLE WIDE WORLD
           FOR ONE HOUR OF LOVE WITH YOU.

           (*Dance.*)

           I'D GIVE THE FLOWERS FROM THE FAIREST OF BOWERS
           I'D GIVE THE GREAT SKY OF BLUE.
           I'D GIVE THE JOYS OF THE WHOLE WIDE WORLD
           FOR ONE HOUR OF LOVE WITH YOU.

(***FSQ.4A; LXQ.9***)

JILL: But where's father? Why hasn't he come to meet me? I
           can't wait to see his kindly, smiling face.

BILLY: I can't wait to see the back of his head.

JILL: Don't be silly, Billy – he's one of the best.

BILLY: You must be ill, Jill – he's a terrible pest.

JACK: You'd better prepare yourself for a shock, Jill. Your father's
           a changed man.

BILLY: And not for the better.

JACK:	He's become terribly greedy . . .
VILLAGER A:	And grasping . . .
VILL. B:	And grumpy . . .
JILL:	But Daddy is the nicest, kindest, gentlest, most generous old softy that you could ever . . .
SQUIRE:	(*Roars off*) CONSTABLE . . . !
JACK:	Look out . . .
BILLY:	Oh no . . .
SQUIRE:	(*Entering from RC, kicking a VILLAGER*) Out of my way, you puerile little poor person . . .
VILL. C:	Do you mind?
SQUIRE:	So! There you are, Constable. Idling as usual. Have you proclaimed my proclamation?
BILLY:	I was just going to, Squire . . .
JILL:	Father . . . ?
SQUIRE:	(*Pushing her away*) Not now, girl. What have you been doing all this time? (*Shaking BILLY.*) You brainless, bootless blithering booby.
BILLY:	It's no use trying to get round me.
JACK:	That's enough of that, Squire. I suggest you leave Billy alone.
VILL. D:	Yes. Leave him alone.
VILL. E:	(*The smallest*) Pick on somebody your own size.
SQUIRE:	And I suggest you keep your nose out of it – all of you. Today is rent day and not one of you is paid up to date. You're all behind.
	(*Everybody looks behind them.*)
SQUIRE:	From now on, anyone falling behind with their rent will be turned out of their house immediately . . .

BILLY: Shame!

SQUIRE: By the Constable . . .

BILLY: Shame . . .

SQUIRE: That's you, you fool . . .

BILLY: That *is* a shame . . .

SQUIRE: And driven from the parish. We'll have no paupers here on pain of the pillory.

JACK: But, Squire, Mother Goose is behind with the rent.

SQUIRE: Precisely. She can be the first to go.

JACK: But we've tried everything to raise the money. Mother Goose is down at the the Galleries now – trying to sell Priscilla's eggs . . .

SQUIRE: Priscilla! You mean that bird-brained moth-eaten old goose? You'd be lucky if she laid one egg a month.

VILL. F: She's not bird-brained.

VILL. G: She's bright.

VILL. H: And beautiful.

VILL. I: And clever.

JACK: And she's a very good layer.

BILLY: Yeh. The other day, she laid a table.

SQUIRE: Well, I'll be generous. I'll give you until two o'clock today. If I haven't received the rent by then, it's out of the house you go.

JILL: Oh, Father, what's come over you? You never used to be so mean and grasping.

SQUIRE: No. I was a buffoon before but now, thanks to my good friend – Mephisto . . .

JILL: Mephisto?!?

(A very dramatic chord.)

ALL: *(Horrified)* Mephisto?!?

SQUIRE: I've seen the error of my ways. Thanks to him, I can see how these peasants have been taking advantage of me. Most of all, that ratbag of a Mother Goose.

JILL: Father. Mother Goose is your oldest friend – and you know that Jack and I are to be married.

SQUIRE: Married? What? To him? Son of a common-or-garden old goose-woman? Never! You're to marry a rich and famous man – my very good friend – the greatest magician in the world . . .

BILLY: Oh no! Not . . . ?

SQUIRE: Yes. Mephisto!

(A very dramatic chord.)

BILLY: Oh, what a relief. I thought he meant Paul Daniels.

JACK: Mephisto?

JILL: Mephisto? Never! Jack . . .

JACK: Don't worry, Jill. I won't let that happen . . .

JILL: You can't make me marry against my will.

SQUIRE: Oh yes I can.

VILLAGERS: Oh no you can't.

SQUIRE: Oh yes I can.

ALL: Oh no you can't.

SQUIRE: You're but a child and mine to dispose of as I please. *(To JACK.)* And you – stay away from my daughter or the constable here'll chuck you in the clink.

JACK: Squire, you may throw us out of our house.

SQUIRE: I shall . . .

JACK: You may drive us from the City.

SQUIRE: I shall . . .

JACK: But Jill will only marry that evil man over my dead body.

SQUIRE: I'm sure that can be arranged. Two o'clock. Tell Mother Goose. Or I'll chuck the pair of you out of this charming cottage. Ha! Ha ha ha . . . Out of my way, you pongy little poor people . . . (*He exits DR.*)

JILL: But . . . Father . . . I . . . (*Weeping.*) Oh, Jack . . . What's to become of us?

JACK: Never fear, Jill.

VILL. A: Don't cry, Jill . . .

JACK: Mother Goose and I will look after you. Even if we all have to become beggars together.

(*JACK and the VILLAGERS crowd round to comfort her.*)

BILLY: (*To the AUDIENCE*) I'm fed up with this Bobbyjob already. I'm going to turn in me truncheon. Hang up me handcuffs. I mean . . . How can I turn Mother Goose out of her windmill? She's my best friend. She's been ever so good to me. She always makes sure I get a good breakfast – muesli – and there's always a second Alpen. And when I had a headcold, she stopped it going onto my chest. She tied a knot in my neck.

(*Music.*) (*LXQ.10*)

JACK: Here she comes now. Back from the Market . . .

JILL: Perhaps she's been able to raise the rent . . .

(*MOTHER GOOSE enters at speed from UL. She is "riding" a Goose. This is a costume/prop with dummy legs over the sides and a flexible neck which she can manouvre in all directions (to "goose" people). Her skirt is tucked up inside the body and she wears "goose feet".*)

MOTHER G: Hello, you tinkers – it's me – Mother Goose – Queen of Cotham. What d'you think of this then? My Goosemobile. Go eighty miles on on a packet of birdseed and a millet spray. But the feathers don't half tickle your comfort zone. I hope I'm not late. I'm just back from the pancake-tossing in Cowes. (*Climbing out and giving the GOOSE to the VILLAGERS.*) Now you just take this off and plug it into recharge, my darling . . . I've just been up the market to sell me eggs. But it's no good – there's too many eggs – a overlay. The bottom's dropped right out of eggs. You've heard of the butter mountain and the wine lake – this is an egg custard.

JACK: But the Squire's only given us 'til two o'clock. What will we do about the rent?

MOTHER G: I don't know. But I've not got no time to worry about it this minute. I've to weed me perennials and feed the animals. Now go mix the mash.

JACK: Alright, Mother (*He goes off sadly DR.*)

MOTHER G: Though where I'll find food to feed the animals after today, I just don't . . . (*To the AUDIENCE.*) Oh hello, you tinkers. You're a nice-looking lot of assorted allsorts. Hello, boys and girls. Mother Goose here of Goose Cottage, Goose Lane, Cotham. Oh, what a situation I'm in – threatened with eviction. Going to be thrown out. Dumped. Mother Goose dumped on the waste tip of life. Not a friend in the world. Except for my dear son, Jack and, of course, my beloved goose, Priscilla. There was a time when I had hundreds of friends. They all liked me at school. I was teacher's pet. She couldn't afford a dog. When I left school – Westbury Park – my mother said "For goodness sake, learn a business so we'll know what sort of work you're out of." But times is hard, dears, times is hard. A man stopped me only the other day – said he hadn't had a bite for three days. So I bit him. And I had to go to the doctor the other day – I said "I find it hard to breathe, Doctor." He said "Are you choking?" I said "No I'm serious." Marvelous the NHS now though. So improved. People are queueing up to use it. Here, I got some lovely presents for Christmas though . . . (*Producing a Water Pistol.*) I got this water pistol. Haven't had time to try it yet. I wonder if it works? (*She squirts the AUDIENCE.*) Ooo it does, doesn't it? But not very well. I did get another water pistol actually as well . . . (*Bringing on a "Super-Soaker".*) Now I wonder if this . . . Hasta la vista, baby . . . Ooo, it does . . . (*Squirting the AUDIENCE.*) I wonder if it works over here as well . . . And what about over here? And up there? Good isn't it? I know . . . (*Going to the proscenium DL.*) D'you want to see what else I got?

(She brings on a full-sized Fire Hose.) No . . . I'll save that for later. Oooh. I nearly forgot . . . got some little eggs for you . . . Priscilla's rejects – I tell you, she lays these like buckshot . . . Would you like some? *(She throws Chocolate Eggs out to the AUDIENCE.)* Now . . . must feed the animals. And you must meet Priscilla – my own very special goose and very best friend in all the world . . . Are you in there, Priscilla . . . ? *(The Stable Door of the Cottage opens and PRISCILLA peeps out.)* Don't be shy. Say hello to the boys and girls.

PRISCILLA: *(To the AUDIENCE)* HONK HONK.

MOTHER G: That's hello in Goose.

PRISCILLA: *(To MOTHER GOOSE)* HONK HONK HONK HONK.

MOTHER G: Oh . . .

PRISCILLA: HONK HONK-HONK HONK.

MOTHER G: Well fancy that. Now let's get this windmill going. *(Calling off R.)* Billy!

BILLY: *(Enters from R)* Coming.

MOTHER G: Well, come on – haven't got all day. Get it going . . .

BILLY: Willco . . .

(He goes US to the windmill and makes fairly ineffectual efforts to turn the sails.)

MOTHER G: That's no good. *(To the AUDIENCE.)* Not enough wind. You'll have to blow . . . You know how to blow don't you? Come on then – blow . . .

(The AUDIENCE start blowing but still nothing happens. During this, the dummy of BILLY is being attached to the offstage sail.)

MOTHER G: Come on. Harder . . .

(The Windmill turns with BILLY (apparently) stuck on the sail.)

BILLY: Aaaah! He-e-elp!

MOTHER G: Billy! Stop that!

BILLY: Aaaaahhhh!

             (*BILLY disappears from the sails. There is a cry and a loud CRASH off R.*)

MOTHER G: Ooops!

             (*Music: intro.*)

             Oh never mind. Come on, all of you.

(*LXQ.11; FSQ.5*)

             Song: DAME SONG (*Whatever is currently popular – possibly with a Line-Dance involving the VILLAGERS*)

             (*During the last chorus of which the cottage pivots to downstage centre to reveal:*)

(*LXQ.12; FSQ.5A*)

                          Scene Three

Interior of MOTHER GOOSE'S Cottage. There is a rocking chair LC, a table C with a cloth to the floor (concealing the egg-machine mechanism), a high cupboard R, steps leading up from C to PRISCILLA'S basket over the cupboard. There is a Sheilamaid hanging from a ceiling beam RC and a little wooden chandelier hanging C.

MOTHER G: Oh it's been a tough day. It was so busy at the market even the Goose asked to come home. Oh . . . Woe is me. I can't pay the rent. And I got held up on the way home – watching the Vicar wash his aspidistra. Then the postman stopped me with a letter. Where's it to, Priscilla? You hiding it? You . . . NAUGHTY NAUGHTY GOOSE!

             (*PRISCILLA gives her the letter.*)

MOTHER G: It's from our Gertrude. I always call her Gert and I leave out the rude bit. Mind you she is gert really. Gert big. Ooooh. She – is – BIG! Massive. It was her birthday last week. I sent her a hula hoop and she's written a thank you letter. "Dear Mother Goose. Thank you for the lovely bracelet – I told you she was big – lovely bracelet you sent me to wear on my P.T.O.

PRISCILLA: HONK HONK HONK-HONK.

MOTHER G: Please turn over? Oh yes. I wear it on my please turnover.

PRISCILLA: HONK HONK HONK HONK-HONK.

MOTHER G: Oh, turn over the paper? Oh yes. I wear it on my . . . wrist. We have just moved into a new home in Pill – just a box really – but it's home. It's very near the gasworks and we get a terrible smell from your ever loving sister Gertrude. PS: If I'm not in bed by 11.30, I'm going home." (*Cuddling PRISCILLA.*) Oh, isn't she lovely? She's the apple of my eye. I got her from Granny Smith. And she's been with me since she was a gosling, haven't you? – just an egg on a plate, weren't you darling? What time is it? (*PRISCILLA taps out three. JACK knocks three times on the door.*) Oh! Six o'clock already.

JACK: (*Entering*) Mother. Billy's coming to throw us out. We'll have to do what he says. It's the law.

MOTHER G: I'm not giving up like that, Jack.

JACK: What if he tries to take Priscilla?

MOTHER G: Over my dead body. If he lays a finger on a feather, I'll flatten his flipping floggel-fluter.

JACK: What's a flipping floggel-fluter?

MOTHER G: I don't know but it sounds painful and it starts with F.

(*PRISCILLA Honks anxiously. BILLY enters, carrying a laundry basket.*)

MOTHER G: Well? What is it, Billy?

BILLY: I'm sorry, Mother Goose but you've got to go. To vamoose.

MOTHER G: To vamoose? With a goose?

BILLY: I have orders from the Squire to remove your removables and repossess your possessions.

MOTHER G: Remove my removables and repossess my possessibles?

BILLY: I have to take away from here goods and chattels to the value of twenty-three thousand pounds, three shillings and fourpence.

MOTHER G: What's the fourpence for?

BILLY: Stamp duty.

MOTHER G: What's stamp duty?

(*He stamps on her foot. BILLY laughs. PRISCILLA stamps on his foot.*)

BILLY: Aaah! But enough of this. (*Taking the Vase from the shelf.*) Now we'll start with this vase . . . this looks about twenty p.

MOTHER G: Twenty p? That's my favourite varse.

BILLY: Varse? You mean Vase.

MOTHER G: I mean varse.

JACK: No, Mother, you mean vawse, as in "because".

BILLY: No. She means Vase – as in "glaze".

MOTHER G: No I don't. I mean varse – as in . . . "Varse"!

BILLY: Well whatever. One vase varse or vawse – twenty p. Right. (*To JACK.*) You write this down. (*Taking Kettle.*) One kettle with spout. (*He packs it into the Basket.*)

JACK: (*Writing*) One kettle with spout.

BILLY: (*Picking up broken Teapot*) One teapot without.

JACK: One teapot without.

BILLY: One brush with handle.

JACK: One brush with handle.

BILLY: One stick with candle.

JACK: One stick with candle.

BILLY: (*With Hot-water Bottle*) One rubber hottie.

JACK: One rubber hottie.

BILLY: (*With Potty*) One potty for the botty.

JACK: One potty for the – do we have to do this?

BILLY: Yes. (*With Ornament.*) One rather nice piece of Rockingham china with ormolu filigree and a delicately raised embossed engraving.

JACK: One rather nice . . .

MOTHER G: Just a minute. Just a minute. Just a minute. This is out of order. You can't take this.

BILLY: Oh yes I can and I will. *And* this. (*Picks up Garden Gnome.*)

BOTH: Oh no! (*Snatching it from him.*) Not the gnome! Are we to be homeless and gnomeless?

BILLY: (*Snatching it back*) Not only the gnome – but also that chandelier.

MOTHER G: Not the chandelier. I've had it since it was a nightlight.

BILLY: Eighty p if we're lucky.

MOTHER G: Well, iron me petty and starch me knickers, it's disgraceful.

BILLY: Never mind all that. On we go. (*With Sheets.*) One pair of sheets – Got them down?

JACK: One pair of sheets – got them down.

BILLY: (*With Slippers*) One pair of slippers. Got them down?

JACK: One pair of slippers. Got them down.

BILLY: (*With Trousers*) One pair of trousers. Got them down?

JACK: One pair of . . . got them down.

BILLY: Well pull 'em up, you're a big boy now.

JACK: You can't do this to us, Billy. We've lived here for years. It's our home. And you're supposed to be our friend.

BILLY: (*Suddenly ashamed and on the verge of tears*) I know I know. I don't want to do it – but it's my duty . . .

JACK: Well . . . I'm (*Turning his back on BILLY.*) disappointed in you . . .

BILLY: (*Tearfully*) Oh no. don't say that . . .

MOTHER G: So'm, I. (*Turning her back.*) Deeply disappointed and . . . and proper let down!

BILLY: (*Sobbing*) Oh no. Oh no. It's no use. I can't do it . . . Unpack all the packables tear up the list. I haven't got it in me . . .

MOTHER G: There there, don't cry. Before we get chucked out, I'll cook us the best spread you ever sprayed. I'll cook you up a lovely little fantailwaterabbit pie and chips. Funnybunny pie they call it. I might even look you out a sausage.

(*PRISCILLA Honks.*)

MOTHER G: What's that dear?

PRISCILLA: HONK HONK HONK-HONK HO-NK . . . !

MOTHER G: Oh . . . You want to lay an egg for Billy? Oh you little darlin'. Would you like an egg, Billy?

BILLY: Oh I'd love an egg – boiled, scrambled, poached or fried.

MOTHER G: Well, Priscilla says she'll drop one for you.

PRISCILLA: HONK. (*And settles for the drop.*)

MOTHER G: Easy gal. Come on now. Relax. Breathe with it.

(*After honks, grunts, strains and waddles, PRISCILLA lays an egg.*)

JACK: That's a whopper, Mum. It's the finest free range egg I've ever seen.

MOTHER G: Oh she can lay eggs, can't you darling? If I could pay the rent with eggs, we'd be quids in – I mean we'd be eggs in – no worries. But, as it is, we . . . (*Breaking down – very dramatic.*) Oh . . . ! No No . . . !

BILLY: No?

MOTHER G: No no no! It's no use . . . I just can't keep going no longer
              . . . I've fought and I've struggled all me life – I've kept me
              nose to the grindstone, me shoulder to the wheel, me fingers
              to the bone and me upper lip stiff – and very uncomfortable
              it's been, I can tell you. But now . . . but now . . . I can't go
              on!

JACK: (*Going to comfort her*) Oh . . . Mother . . . !

BILLY: (*Sobbing*) Neither can I . . .

JACK: Oh, Billy . . .

MOTHER G: The buffets and billows of life have battered me bonnet and
              banjaxed me bonhommie . . . I – can't – go – ON! (*She
              collapses onto the stool upstage of the table and beats her
              fists on the table.*)

BILLY: (*Breaking down*) Neither can I, Mother Goose. Oh . . .
              Woe! Neither can I! I – can't – go – ON! (*Collapses onto
              the stool L and beats his fists on the table.*)

JACK: (*Trying to comfort both of them*) Oh come on now . . . Cheer
              up, both of you . . . Oh! (*Breaking down.*) Neither can I . . . !
              I – can't – go – ON! (*He collapses onto the stool R of the
              table and beats his fists.*)

ALL: (*In rhythm*) We – can't – go – ON!

              (*PRISCILLA runs up and down, flapping her wings and
              honking in distress. There is a Flash DL (Pyro Q.4;
              LXQ.13; FSQ.6) and all but PRISCILLA freeze as
              MEPHISTO appears DL. PRISCILLA honks and cowers
              away.*)

MEPHISTO: (*To the AUDIENCE*) Didn't I tell you? Didn't I say?
              That I would have my wicked way?
              Now poverty will lead her into crime and selfishness and
                                                              trickery.
              She'll be bad-tempered all the time and snappy, mean and
                                                              bickery
              Then she'll be just as I like folks to be – cheating, sly and
                                                              thieving –
              But then, you needn't stay to see. You might as well be
                                                              leaving.

(There is a FLASH DR. **(PyroQ.5; LXQ.14; FSQ.7)** *FAIRY GOOSEFEATHER appears.)*

FAIRY: *(Covering the AUDIENCE with her wand – TV Police style)*
                 Freeze! Nobody move. Everyone stay seated.
                 Until this monster is defeated.
                 (To MEPHISTO.) You thoroughly bad sort! You beastly
                                                                      thing!
                 You ornithological demon king!
                 How dare you work for her discredit?
                 You wretch! You . . . Cad! There now, I've said it.

MEPHISTO: Sticks and stones
                 Have never been known to shatter my repose
                 I'm quite impervious to names.

FAIRY: You get right up my nose.
                 But I will thwart you – wait and see.
                 Mother Goose is safe with me.

MEPHISTO: Well you can help her if you like
                 And that foolish lover, Jack.

FAIRY: Be off, Mephisto. On your bike.

MEPHISTO: Very well. But I'll be back!

                 (There is a Flash DR **(PyroQ.6; LXQ.15; FSQ.6A)** *and MEPHISTO disappears. PRISCILLA honks and cuddles up to FAIRY GOOSEFEATHER, very distressed.)*

FAIRY: Don't fret, Priscilla, you will see
                 That all will turn out happilee.
                 I'll put my magic spells to use
                 And make of you a magic goose.

PRISCILLA: HONK?

FAIRY: You want to help her?

PRISCILLA: HONK.

FAIRY: Though it may be hard?

PRISCILLA: HONK HONK.

FAIRY: Then you shall be her credit card.

PRISCILLA: HONK?

FAIRY: Her debts you'll settle in the end – whatever the amount.
              You'll be her feathered flexible friend – her Premium Gold
              account.

              *(She waves her wand elaborately and then touches
              PRISCILLA with it. **(LXQ.16; PyroQ.7)** There is a Flash
              C. PRISCILLA jumps in the air, spins round a few times,
              falls over, gets up, bangs her ear with her wing and
              becomes instantly broody.)*

FAIRY: There now. That's done.
              Gosh! Spells are fun – but I can't hang about.
              He's boobed again
              At number ten –
              I'd better help him out.

              *(Flash DR **(PyroQ.8; FSQ.7A; LXQ.17)** and she
              disappears. JACK and BILLY wake with a start.)*

JACK: What's that? What's happened.

BILLY: *(Hugging the Gnome)* No, Madonna, I won't marry you . . .
              (Waking properly.) Oh!

              (MOTHER GOOSE snores on.)

JACK: Wake up, Mother.

MOTHER G: Yes your Highness. The negatives are safe with me. Oh. I
              was having a wonderful dream. I dreamt I was Queen for a
              day. I was paying taxes and showing people over my home.
              I must've been dreaming.

JACK: Oh, Mother. You're always dreaming.

MOTHER G: Dreams is all we've got left now. Come on. Let's get that
              egg cooked for Billy.

PRISCILLA: HONK HONK.

MOTHER G: Oh gracious me. She wants to drop another. That's two in
              a day. It must've been something she ate.

              (PRISCILLA is shimmying about and straining.)

MOTHER G:	What is it you want, dear? Neurophen or WD 40? Come on now. Easy does it. Steady now. Steady past your grannies ... Oh ... like liquid engineering ...

(PRISCILLA gives a honk of relief as a golden egg drops with a thud.)

MOTHER G: Oh you clever girl. That *is* a big one. We should enter it for the Bath and West Show. It's magnificent.

JACK: But, Mother, that's no *ordinary* egg ...

MOTHER G: Does look a bit odd and *(Picking it up with two hands)* ... Oh! Weighs a ton ...

JACK: Odd? It's ... GOLD!

MOTHER G: Gold?

BILLY: She must've been at the Golden Wonder crisps.

MOTHER G: Well snap me beads and diddle me elastic. It *is* gold. You clever girl, Priscilla. I'll be able to pay the rent now.

PRISCILLA: BROODY HONK.

JACK: What? Another?

(PRISCILLA nods violently and strains.)

BILLY: Oh another gold one. Go for it, Prissy. Go for gold.

MOTHER G: Steady. Don't strain too much gal, you might crack it.

(PRISCILLA, after much straining lays another (larger) Golden Egg. They all cheer.)

BILLY: It's enormous.

MOTHER G: Oooh, it's a good job they're not square.

BILLY: Is it really gold, Mother Goose?

MOTHER G: *(Picking it up with great difficulty)* It looks like gold and it's heavy enough for gold and it's all smoothe and slippery like gold ...

BILLY: But is it solid?

(*The egg slips from MOTHER GOOSE'S hands and drops on BILLY'S foot.*)

BILLY: Aaaah!

MOTHER G: Seems to be.

PRISCILLA: HONKS AND BROODY AGAIN.

JACK: She wants to do it again, Mother. Fantastic.

BILLY: Oh no. This is getting out of hand.

MOTHER G: It's getting out of somewhere.

BILLY: She hasn't got it in her.

MOTHER G: She won't have in a minute. Brace yourself, gal. Now come on don't look. Get some purchase dear. Get a good grip on the tufted shag.

(*More straining, honking and flapping accompanied by a roll of drums and cymbal crash as PRISCILLA lays a huge golden egg.*)

JACK: That's the biggest yet.

BILLY: She must be egg-sausted . . .

JACK: Are you alright, Priscilla?

PRISCILLA: (*Happily exhausted*) HONK!

MOTHER G: We're rich. We're rich!

BILLY: You'll be able to pay the rent now, Mother Goose. You can have anything you want. You can have a Porsche. You can have a credit card at Debenhams, You could even afford a cup of tea at the Swallow Royal Hotel.

MOTHER G: Cup of tea nothing. I shall be able to buy the Swallow Royal. I shall call it the Goose Royale . . .

JACK: Oh, Mother, you're not going to get delusions of grandeur, are you?

MOTHER G:	I shall certainly want to broaden my horizons. Take out some PEPS and Tessas. Just think – we could leave the cottage – move into a nice semi – or a little Barratt's house – or a small palace, who knows?
JACK:	But we've always been happy here.
MOTHER G:	Oh yes. I'm quite happy here – with the damp, the blocked drains, the endless bills. Oh, I don't know. Perhaps I could face life in a palace.
JACK:	Oh, Mother, isn't it wonderful. Jill and I can be married . . .
MOTHER G:	I'm speechless with emotion . . .
PRISCILLA:	(*Broody again*) HONK!
BILLY:	And Priscilla's back in motion. Look out . . .

(*PRISCILLA lays a small golden egg.*)

MOTHER G:	Another one!

(*PRISCILLA lays another one.*)

JACK:	And another.
MOTHER G:	We won't be able to cope if she doesn't stop . . .
JACK:	We'll have to get organised. Come on. Let's set up a production line. Up on your nest, Priscilla . . .

(*PRISCILLA climbs up onto her nest.*)

JACK:	(*Lowering the Sheilamaid to preset angle – to lead from under the nest to the top of the table*) This'll make a chute, mother – for the eggs to roll down . . .
MOTHER G:	We need a conveyor belt . . . (*She takes off her corset and, masking the table with her skirt – apparently – rigs it as a conveyor belt.*)
BILLY:	(*Arranging drainpipes and guttering*) I'll get help. (*Calling off.*) Hey, Jill . . . Boys and girls. Come and help Jack and Mother Goose.

(*JILL and the VILLAGERS rush in.*)

JILL: What's going on?

                 (*Music: intro.*) (***LXQ.18***)

JACK: I'll explain later. Here – give me a hand, Jill . . .

                 To: "GOOSE GOOSE GOOSE GOOSE GOOSEY, LAY A
                 LITTLE EGG FOR ME", *PRISCILLA lays a steady stream of
                 eggs which fall through the trap under her nest, roll down
                 the Sheilamaid, along the corset conveyer belt, along a
                 length of guttering, to be flipped by BILLY'S ladle back
                 across to the VILLAGERS who catch them, pack them into
                 baskets and carry them off.* (***SQ.3***) *There is an Easter egg,
                 a fried egg, etc. The last egg is picked up by MOTHER
                 GOOSE. It hatches a little fluffy chick.*)

ALL: AAAWWW!

                 (*Blackout.*)   (***LXQ.19; Fly Q.2***)

(***LXQ.20***)

                              Scene Four

Frontcloth. Lover's Lane. A Flash DL. (***PyroQ.9; SQ.4***) *A Crash of
thunder. MEPHISTO appears, basking in Lightning.*

MEPHISTO: The lightning splits the heavens assunder –
                 Torrential rain and cracking good thunder –
                 That's why I'm happy – so chuffed – so gay –
                 It's truly a Mephisto sort of day!

                 (*A Flash DR. FAIRY GOOSEFEATHER appears, bringing
                 instant sunshine* (***LXQ.21***) *and the twittering of song-birds*
                 (***SQ.5***) *to her side of the stage.*)

FAIRY: Oh no it's not!
                 What tommyrot!
                 (*Lyrical.*) See how the sun is shining.
                 The bees hum loud
                 And every cloud
                 Hangs out its silver lining.
                 Bluebirds fly over
                 Fields of clover
                 And every little chick
                 Is twee and cute in his little fluffy suit . . .

MEPHISTO: Excuse me while I'm sick!

FAIRY: You're only jealous –
No need to tell us –
Because I spoiled your spell . . .

MEPHISTO: On the contrary,
You foolish fairy,
I'm doing rather well.
You've done my work,
You Fairy . . . burk!
By making Mother Goose rich.
When poor she could
Tell bad from good
Now she don't know which is which.
Money is sure
To corrupt the pure . . .

FAIRY: No!

MEPHISTO: As certain as eggs is eggs.

FAIRY: No!

MEPHISTO: Wait and see . . .

FAIRY: It cannot be!
You really are the dregs!

MEPHISTO: The money is burning her purse, you'll have to get a shift on.
She's gone and bought up Ashton Court and now she's
buying Clift-on!

FAIRY: (*To the AUDIENCE*) Gosh . . . What if I'm wrong and what if
he's right?
Some of us fairies aren't frightfully bright.
I must flit awf and stop and accost her
Before she can get to the Cheltenham and Gloucester.

(*A Flash DR.* (**PyroQ.10; LXQ.22**) *She disappears.
Darkness returns. Thunder rumbles. The SQUIRE enters
from R in a trance. He wears his hat with the Black
Feather.*)

MEPHISTO: Ah here comes my slave. Welcome, Squire . . .

SQUIRE: (*Zomboid*) What is your will, O Mighty Nastiness? (*He
prepares to remove his hat and bow.*)

MEPHISTO: *Don't* take off that hat . . .

SQUIRE: A sign of respect, Oh Repellant One . . .

MEPHISTO: I told you. You're to keep the hat on at *all times.* And never never *NEVER* remove the black feather. Now. How dare you come to me alone? I told you to bring your daughter to me today. Churl . . . Where's the girl?

SQUIRE: Forgive me, Oh Doggy Doo. It isn't my fault . . .

MEPHISTO: Not your fault? You promised her to me . . . today.

SQUIRE: Indeed I did, Great Poo-poo, but the girl is in hiding with an unpleasant peasant . . .

MEPHISTO: Peasant? You mean that . . . Jackanapes, I suppose – son of the Goose woman.

SQUIRE: Yes, your Stinkiness . . .

MEPHISTO: Then I command you to find her out and fetch her to me. And while you're about it, get me the goose.

SQUIRE: Goose?

MEPHISTO: Mother Goose's goose. The fowl is laying eggs of gold
And I might as well have my share.
So fetch me the goose and fetch me the girl –
They'll make a delightful pair . . .

SQUIRE: The goose is guarded night and day, Oh Great Sublimest Slime.
Even when she goes out to play, that Jack is with her all the time.

MEPHISTO: Then you go up to him and you repeat this spell:
"What a lovely day. How fine and bright.
Oh! Look up there! And so – Goodnight"
He'll fall asleep and you steal the goose.

SQUIRE: Why will he fall asleep?

MEPHISTO: Because, when he looks up there, (*Producing a massive club from beneath his cloak.*) you hit him – with this. Here. Now practice.

SQUIRE: (*Taking the club*) What a lovely day. How fine and bright.

Oh! Look up there! (*MEPHISTO looks up.*) And so –
GOODNIGHT!

(*The SQUIRE hits him on the head.*)

MEPHISTO: (*Staggering*) Aah! Not me, you fool . . .

SQUIRE: Just practicing, Oh Mighty Midden . . .

MEPHISTO: Well practice on someone else. Now I must fly.
             But bring me my booty bye and bye.

(*An abortive Flash DL (**PyroQ.11**) which only fizzes.*)

MEPHISTO: (*To the Pyro*) I know just how you feel . . . (*He totters off
             DL.*)

SQUIRE: (*Practicing robotically*) What a lovely day. How fine and
             bright.
             Oh! Look up there! And so (*Thumping the floor.*)
             GOODNIGHT!

(*BILLY enters DR.*)

BILLY: Hello, Squire. Have you heard the news about Mother
             Goose?

SQUIRE: (*Approaching him*) What a lovely day . . .

BILLY: Yes it's turned out nice again, hasn't it?

SQUIRE: How fine and bright . . .

BILLY: But you see Mother Goose is rich now and . . .

SQUIRE: Oh! Look up there!

BILLY: (*Taking a pace to one side as he looks up*) Where?

SQUIRE: And so – GOODNIGHT! (*He brings the club down hard on
             the spot where BILLY would have been.*)

BILLY: (*Knocking the SQUIRE'S hat off*) D'you mind? You nearly
             knocked my head off.

SQUIRE: (*Instantly genial*) Well . . . Bless my soul . . . What am I
             doing here? (*Looking at the club in his hand.*) And what
             am I doing with this? Hello, Billy, my dear chap . . .

BILLY: Don't you "dear chap" me. You were going to clobber me with that cudgel 'til I knocked your hat off. (*Inspiration – DING! in the orchestra pit*) The hat! That's it.

SQUIRE: That's what?

BILLY: Mephisto must've bewitched your hat. That's why you've been so nasty all these weeks.

SQUIRE: Have I?

BILLY: You certainly have. Here. Put it on.

(*The SQUIRE puts the hat on and is immediately evil again.*)

SQUIRE: (*Roaring and brandishing the club*) What a lovely day!

BILLY: (*Whipping the hat off him*) Oh no you don't . . .

SQUIRE: (*Genial again*) Why, Billy . . . I keep coming over most peculiar . . .

BILLY: I was right. Mephisto has bewitched your hat. But you'll be alright now, Squire, because I'm going to chuck it away. I'll keep this feather though. I quite like that. There we are. Good riddance! (*He throws the hat off stage and puts the feather in his lapel. He undergoes an immediate personality change.*)

SQUIRE: Well, I must say. I feel a lot better now. Without that hat, eh, Billy, I say . . .

BILLY: (*Brandishing the club*) What a lovely day . . . !

SQUIRE: Oh no!

(*He runs off DL, pursued by BILLY.*)

(LXQ.23; SQ.6)

(*JACK and JILL enter hand in hand DR.*)

JILL: Oh, Jack, I'm so happy. My Father can't stop us marrying now – not now that Mother Goose is so rich.

JACK: Yes. Isn't it wonderful. Though, I must say, I'm a bit
                 worried about Mother Goose. I think all that gold has gone
                 to her head. You know she's bought a palace?

SQUIRE: A palace?

JACK: Huge place. She's holding a great ball there tonight. She's
                 invited just about the whole city . . .

JILL: Oh well, she's worked hard all her life. She deserves a bit of
                 luxury. In any case, nothing can worry me – when we have
                 each other.

PRISCILLA: (*Peeping round the proscenium DR*) HONK.

                 (*Music: intro.*)

BOTH: And Priscilla!

(*LXQ.24; FSQ.8*)

                 Song: PRISCILLA (*JACK, JILL and PRISCILLA – HONKS*)
                 PRISCILLA!
                 SHE'S A FRIEND WHO'S RATHER RARE,
                 SHE'S AS HUGGY AS A BEAR
                 OR A GORILLA.
                 PRISCILLA!
                 LOTS OF HAPPINESS SHE'LL BRING
                 AS WE SAIL THROUGH LIFE, HER WING
                 UPON THE TILLER.
                 WHEN WE'RE FEELING BLUE AND SKIES ARE GREY
                 AND LIFE HAS LOST ALL SENSE OF FUN,
                 WHO'S THE ONE WHO CHASES ALL THE CLOUDS
                 AWAY
                 AND POLISHES UP THE SUN?
                 PRISCILLA!
                 IF WE'D NOTHING LEFT TO SHARE,
                 WE'D BE STILL A MILLIONAIRE
                 AND THAT IS TRUE.
                 WHO'S THE ONE WHO KNOWS THE WAY
                 TO TURN THE DARKEST NIGHT TO DAY?
                 PRISCILLA – YES IT'S YOU.

                 (*Blackout.*)   (*LXQ.25; FSQ.8A*)

(*FlyQ.3; LXQ.26*)

Scene Five

Mother Goose's Palace of Gold. A balcony UC with arches leading to it R and L, also staircases leading down from it R and L to stage level. In front of the balcony C stands the "Tiddlypot". This can be simply a Pot on its side, capable of pouring liquid, or it can be something like a tea-urn OR, ideally, it can be a Greek-type statue bearing a tilted urn on its shoulder and a basket worn on a sling at the hip. The figure wears a loincloth and is operated by a person sitting masked behind it. There is a table R with bowls of cakes, sandwiches and exotic fruit, bottles of wine, glasses and a soda syphon.

Music: intro. A CHORUS of FOOTMEN and PARLOURMAIDS is laying food on the tables while singing and dancing.

CHORUS: OPEN THE WINDOWS, OPEN THE DOOR,
BLOWING ALL THE COBWEBS AND THE DUST AWAY.
POLISH THE CRYSTAL, POLISH THE FLOOR,
THAT WILL KEEP US BUSY PART OF EVERY DAY.
A FEATHER DUSTER
OR BRUSH AND BROOM
WILL BRING BACK LUSTRE
TO EACH AND EVERY MUSTY ROOM.
SO, BRING OUT THE SILVER, TIDY THE DRAWER,
PUT THE SILVER CANDELABRA ON DISPLAY.
EMPTY THE PANTRY, EMPTY THE STORE,
MAKE THE TABLE READY FOR THE FEAST TODAY
AND, WHEN IT'S DONE,
IT'S TIME FOR FUN TO START.
SO LET'S DO IT WITHOUT DELAY
FOR MOTHER GOOSE'S POSH SOIREE.

(During the song, the SQUIRE, PRISCILLA, JACK and JILL enter L.)

(LXQ.27)

(BILLY enters at the top of the stairs.)

BILLY: My lords, ladies and gentlemen. The Right Honourable the Mother Goose of Cotham!

(Fanfare. MOTHER GOOSE enters through the Arch L at the top of the stairs, sending BILLY riccocheting off through the Arch R. She wears an absolutely outrageous ball gown and carries a huge reticule. To music, she descends the staircase graciously until she trips and lands

in a heap at the foot of the stairs. PRISCILLA hurries forward to help her up.)

MOTHER G: Now. (*She is suddenly very posh and full of her own importance.*) There's too much tarradiddle going on here. We must get things organised for the reception. Mother Goose's coming out party.

SQUIRE: Coming out alright.

BILLY: Yeh. She's coming out all over the place.

MOTHER G: I heard that.

JACK: But, Mother! This palace . . . this banquet . . . We don't need it.

MOTHER G: Well I want it. And, with all the golden eggs from Priscilla I can have anything I want. And I intend to. And I want a Nintendo, too. Now come on, you lot – jump to it.

JACK: Oh dear. Mother's acting ever so strangely since she became rich. I don't think this is going to be my sort of party.

JILL: Nor mine.

JACK: Why don't we take Priscilla for a walk by the river?

JILL: Oh yes. Come on, Priscilla . . .

(*They slip away through the door L.*)

MOTHER G: I wonder what's keeping all my posh guests. Oooohh. My, I could murder a pint of Wincarnis. I've a mouth like the bottom of our birdcage. (*Seeing the statue.*) Oh look – a tiddly pot.

SQUIRE: A tiddly pot?

BILLY: A tiddly pot?

MOTHER G: Yes. A tiddly pot.

BOTH: What's a tiddly pot?

MOTHER G: It comes with wealth, dear. All the best people have one. Like tupperware and loose covers. With a tiddly pot, you can have any drink you want anytime you want. With a tiddly pot, you can have a Coke, a Lilt, a Seven-up . . . On a good day – you can even be tangoed.

SQUIRE: Oh yes. Let's tango.

MOTHER G: Not now. Not now.

BILLY: (*Intrigued by it*) Show me how your tiddly pot works, Mother Goose.

MOTHER G: Well, you go up to it and you say: "Tiddly pot, tiddly pot, what have you got for me?

POT: (*SQ.7*) What is your desire?

BILLY: (*To the SQUIRE*) Was that you?

MOTHER G: (*Holding out a glass*) I'll have a Bloody Mary. (*She stamps her foot.*)

POT: (*SQ.8*) Please.

MOTHER G: Please. (*She stamps her foot again.*)

(*A Red Drink is poured into the glass from the Pot.*)

MOTHER G: Cheers. (*She drains the glass.*) You see, it's easy. You have a go.

BILLY: Can I? Can I?

MOTHER G: Yes, Billy, you can.

BILLY: Piddly tot, piddly tot,

MOTHER G: No no . . . tiddly pot, tiddly pot –

BILLY: Piddly tot, piddly tot . . .

MOTHER G: No no . . . Tiddle! Tiddly tiddly pot. Here. Let me show you again. (*Pushing him out of the way.*) Tiddly pot, tiddly pot, what have you got for me?

POT: (*SQ.9*) What is your desire?

MOTHER G: I'll have a double green dry martini. Please. (*She stamps her foot.*)

(*A Green Drink is poured into the glass from the Pot.*)

MOTHER G: With a slice of lemon . . .

(*The Figure lifts a slice of lemon from his basket and drops it into the glass. PLOP.*)

MOTHER G: And an ice cube . . .

(*The same business with an ice cube. PLOP.*)

MOTHER G: And one of those little umbrellas . . .

POT: (*SQ.10*) What do you want the umbrella for?

MOTHER G: To keep the martini dry, nit-wit . . .

(*The same business with a cocktail umbrella. MOTHER GOOSE drains the drink, throwing the additives over her shoulder and burping.*)

BILLY: I've got it. I've got it. Now then. Watch this . . . Tiddly pot, tiddly pot, what have you got for me?

POT: (*SQ.11*) What is your desire?

BILLY: I'll have a double Fanta please.

(*Nothing happens.*)

MOTHER G: (*Getting a bit slurred*) No no let me show you again. Tiddly pot, tiddly pot, what have you got for me?

POT: (*SQ.12*) What is your desire.

MOTHER G: I'll have a gert big double lilt plus a zambouka spritzer and some angosturals, please. (*She stamps her foot.*)

(*A Blue Drink is poured into the glass from the Pot.*)

BILLY: But I did that, didn't I kids?

AUDIENCE: NO.

BILLY: What did I do wrong?

AUDIENCE: YOU DIDN'T STAMP YOUR FOOT.

BILLY:　　　　I've got it. I've got it. Tiddly pot, tiddly pot, what have you got for me?

POT:　　　　(*SQ.13*)　What is your desire?

BILLY:　　　　I'll have a bucket of beer please. (*He stamps his foot.*)

(*The Figure lowers its loincloth and pees a jet of beer into his face.*)

BILLY:　　　　That's not fair. I don't like this game.

(*MOTHER GOOSE and the SQUIRE, laughing, move to the table R.*)

SQUIRE:　　　May I give you some champagne Mother Goose?

MOTHER G:　　Oh yes. I love a bit of a shampoo – some fizz. But not too many bubbles, please, they tickle my snitch.

BILLY:　　　　I've got some fiz, Mother Goose (*Bringing a soda syphon.*) Here we are.

(*He squirts some into her glass.*)

MOTHER G:　　Oh thank you so much, Billy.

SQUIRE:　　　Give me some of that, would you?

BILLY:　　　　(*He looks at the AUDIENCE*) Shall I?　(*He squirts the SQUIRE in the face.*)

SQUIRE:　　　Well! I like that.

MOTHER G:　　You heard him. He liked it. Give him some more.

(*BILLY squirts the SQUIRE again and then staggers about the stage, laughing helplessly. MOTHER GOOSE opens her handbag and takes out a funnel attached to a length of piping. She mimes her plan to the SQUIRE and, together, they steer BILLY to stand along side the Tiddly Pot. MOTHER GOOSE inserts the pipe down the front of his trousers while the SQUIRE holds the funnel under the Tiddly Pot. BILLY begins to look uneasy.*)

SQUIRE:　　　Tiddly pot, tiddly pot, what have you got for me?

POT: *(SQ.14)* What is your desire?

SQUIRE: Fill it up and give me the stamps. Er . . . what do I do now?

AUDIENCE: STAMP.

SQUIRE: Shall I?

AUDIENCE: Yes.

(*The SQUIRE stamps. BILLY shakes and gurgles as the pot fills him up. When he is full, a bell rings. BILLY rolls and wobbles about the stage. MOTHER GOOSE and the SQUIRE are roaring with laughter. BILLY produces a hot water bottle from his trousers, pulls a face at them and runs off.*)

(*Music: Tango.*) **(*LXQ.28*)**

MOTHER G: Oh, Squire – It's "Come Dancing".

SQUIRE: I know.

MOTHER G: I know you know.

SQUIRE: I know you know I know.

MOTHER G: Let's Tango.

(*Tango routine. MOTHER GOOSE takes a flower from a vase on the table R and sticks it between her teeth, she whips the cloth off, leaving all the banquet items behind, puts a confection of fruit on her head and taunts the SQUIRE like a matador. The SQUIRE grabs two bananas from the table L and charges as a bull. This turns into a cod tango which leads to a big finish as both end up on the floor.*)

(*LXQ.29*)

SQUIRE: (*Getting up, yawning*) Oh! It's no good, Mother Goose. I'm off to bed. It must be two in the morning.

MOTHER G: But why hasn't nobody come to my party? I invited all the nobs. Why didn't they come?

SQUIRE: I reckon they think we're a bit common.

MOTHER G: Common? Living in a palace? Common?

SQUIRE: Never mind.

MOTHER G: But I do mind. I mind very much, mind . . .

SQUIRE: Well . . . I'm sorry, Mother Goose, but I'm off to bed.
Goodnight.

*(He goes wearily up the stairs L and exits through the UL
Arch.   MOTHER GOOSE sits sadly on the stairs R.
PRISCILLA enters at UR Arch and comes down the stairs to
comfort her.)*

MOTHER G: Oh, I dunno, Priscilla. What a let down. My coming out
party and nobody come to see me fall out . . .

(The Door L creaks open.)

MOTHER G: *(To PRISCILLA)* You'd better have some Alka Seltzer with
your next bowl of bread crumbs . . .

*(MEPHISTO enters through the door.   He gestures and it
creaks shut behind him.)*

MEPHISTO: Dear lady . . .

MOTHER G: Oh. A guest. He looks ever so posh. Must be a lord of
some sort. Good evening, sir. Are you one of the
aristosprats?

MEPHISTO: *(Sweeping round in a circle swirling his cloak)* I certainly
move in the very best circles . . .

MOTHER G: Then, if you're in the best circles, why hasn't nobody else
come round? Why did nobody come to my ball?

MEPHISTO: *(Suave)* May I speak frankly?

MOTHER G: Pray do, Frank.

MEPHISTO: May I tell you what only your best friend can tell you?

MOTHER G: Well, don't look like I've got no other friends.

MEPHISTO: Can you take it?

MOTHER G: Course I can take it. Look at this figure – 38-26-38 and
wouldn't I half make you jump. Here's me – done up lovely
as a lampshade from British Home Stores . . .

MEPHISTO: Then the truth is . . .

MOTHER G: What?

MEPHISTO: No no, I can't . . . I don't want to hurt you . . .

MOTHER G: Tell me . . . Tell me . . .

MEPHISTO: But the truth is very . . . painful.

MOTHER G: Well . . . you could lie a bit . . .

MEPHISTO: I cannot lie –
No no, not I.
I'm truthful and fastidious.
So to hell with tact,
It's a well-known fact –
You're absolutely hideous.

MOTHER G: *(Faints and falls down)* Ah!

MEPHISTO: Are you upset?

MOTHER G: No . . .

MEPHISTO: Up you get . . .

MOTHER G: *(Struggling up)* I'm . . . *ugly* . . . do you mean?

MEPHISTO: You've the sort of face
Found in outer space –
Very useful for Hallowe'en .

MOTHER G: *(Snatches up a hand mirror and looks at herself)*
Wrinkle, wrinkle,little star –
Hope they never see the scar. *(The mirror shatters into
fragments. She swoons again.)* Ah!

MEPHISTO: You're a blight.
You're a fright.
You're a terrible sight
To encounter after dark.
You're mistaken for
A dinosaur –

Escaped from Jurassic Park.

(*MOTHER GOOSE is crawling round the floor, wailing and beating her head.*)

MEPHISTO: Have I been tactless? Have I said too much?

MOTHER G: (*Hurt*) Is that really how folk see me?

MEPHISTO: You've all the charm
Of a sewage farm
And a face like a JCB.
You're as slack as a sack of wet cement
You're as lumpy as lard or suet.
You're like Dr Frankenstein's first attempt
Before he learned how to do it.

MOTHER G: What can I do?

MEPHISTO: Let *me* help you. Dear lady, depend on me . . .
I can re-lay you,
Remould and respray you.
You'll be lovely – just wait and you'll see.

MOTHER G: But . . . who *are* you?

MEPHISTO: Mephisto the beautician – cosmetic surgeon to the stars.
I can make you beautiful – in all part-ic-u-lars.

MOTHER G: You can?

MEPHISTO: You'll be transformed. You'll be translated
To the loveliest creature ever created

MOTHER G: I will?

MEPHISTO: You'll be the theme
Of every man's dream –
Whether film star, King or beggar.
At every premiere . . .

MOTHER G: Will *I* be there?

MEPHISTO: With Arnold Schwarzenegar.
You'll be lovely.

MOTHER G: (*Rhapsodic*) I'll be lovely . . . ! Oh, tell me what to do . . .

MEPHISTO: You have only to bathe in my Magic Waterfall and you will be a new woman. Mind . . . It'll cost you. It don't come cheap.

MOTHER G: I don't care what it costs. I've always wanted to be beautiful more than anything . . .

MEPHISTO: More than . . . anything?

MOTHER G: More than anything in the world. What do I do?

MEPHISTO: Here. (*He allows a very long roll of paper to unroll – very like a toilet roll.*) Just sign this contract . . .

MOTHER G: (*Feeling it*) It's soft . . .

MEPHISTO: And strong . . .

MOTHER G: And very very long . . .

MEPHISTO: (*He pulls a quill from his cloak. A "Pop" in orchestra pit.*) Ouch! (*Giving it to her.*) Here. Just sign at the bottom . . .

MOTHER G: (*Peering*) You've got very small print on your bottom. But how much?

MEPHISTO: I don't want money.

MOTHER G: (*About to sign*) Oh well that's alright then . . .

MEPHISTO: I'll take . . . (*Looking round elaborately*) let's see now . . . oh . . . the goose.

MOTHER G: (*Freezing*) What?

PRISCILLA: (*Worried*) HONK.

MEPHISTO: (*Evilly*) I'm very fond of animals . . . Surely you've seen me on "Animal Hospital" . . .

MOTHER G: But she's like one of the family . . .

MEPHISTO: Really? which one?

MOTHER G: Look – why don't you . . . take everything else – take the whole palace?

MEPHISTO: No. My mind's made up. It's the goose or nothing . . .

PRISCILLA: (*Plaintive*) HONK.

MOTHER G: Then it'll have to be nothing.

MEPHISTO: (*Rolling up the contract*) Very well. You can remain as you are . . . (*Viciously.*) Ugly . . . !

MOTHER G: Ah!

MEPHISTO: Repulsive . . .

MOTHER G: Ah!

MEPHISTO: Utterly repellent . . . Eaugh . . . !

MOTHER G: No no. Wait a minute . . .

MEPHISTO: (*Half unrolls the contract*) Well?

PRISCILLA: (*Pleading*) HONK. HONK HONK HONK. (*Please don't sign.*)

MOTHER G: No. I can't part with the goose . . .

MEPHISTO: (*Rolling it up again*) Then might I suggest . . . a mask? A paper bag? A tent? The millenium Dome? (*Laughing nastily.*) You . . . gargoyle. You . . . eyesore. You . . . walking nightmare . . .

MOTHER G: (*In tears*) No! No! Don't start again . . . I can't bear it!

MEPHISTO: (*Unrolling the contract – very persuasive – handing her the quill*) Then sign, Mother Goose, sign . . .

PRISCILLA: (*Running about, distressed*) HONK. HONK. HONK.

MOTHER G: Oh shut up, Priscilla. How can I think when you're honkin' all the time?

(*PRISCILLA subsides into sad little squeaks.*)

MEPHISTO: (*Persuasive*) Yes. Think, Mother Goose . . . Think hard. Opportunity never knocks twice. Miss this chance and there'll never be another. Today could be the first day of the rest of your life . . . Think it over . . .

MOTHER G: It's very tempting . . .

PRISCILLA: HONK HONK.

MOTHER G: It's alright for you, Priscilla. You've always been beautiful
– even as an egg – as a little fluffy chick and then, since
you let in your first clutch, you've been as gorgeous a
goose as ever gaggled. Me now – I've always looked like
the back of a bus. See those wrinkles? Badgerline.

PRISCILLA: (*Desperate*) HONK . . . ! HONK . . . !

MOTHER G: Oh stop being so selfish and think of me for once. Don't
you want me to be happy?

PRISCILLA: HONK. (*Yes.*)

MOTHER G: Right then. (*Signing.*) There!

MEPHISTO: (*Snatching the contract away*) Ah ha! Well done.
You'll never regret it.
Now the goose is mine and don't you forget it.
(*Giving her an ornate certificate and heading for the
door.*)
Come along, Goose, and waddle this way –
To my cave in the Gorge. Make no delay . . . (*He exits,
cackling.*)

(*Music: HEARTS AND FLOWERS*) (*LXQ.30*)

PRISCILLA: (*Wailing*) HONK HONK HONK . . .

MOTHER G: It's for the best, Priscilla . . .

PRISCILLA: (*Wailing*) HONK. HONK. HONK.

MOTHER G: It's no use. I don't want you no more. Go. Go on . . . I've
my own life to lead . . . Go away and leave me in peace . . .

(*PRISCILLA moves sadly towards the door.*)

MOTHER G: Just go, Priscilla. Please. Please, my darling. I want so
much to be beautiful and . . . Please GO!

(*LXQ.31*)

(*PRISCILLA reaches the door, turns and looks back at
MOTHER GOOSE.*)

PRISCILLA: HONK HONK (*Good bye.*) HONK HONK HONK HONK-
HONK HONK (*I love you, Mother Goose*).

MOTHER G: I love you too, Priscilla . . . But I . . . want so much to . . . be
beautiful . . .

MEPHISTO: (*Calling from off*) Come on, Goose. Get along with you!

(*PRISCILLA exits, sobbing. The door creaks and slams
shut. The Music swells as MOTHER GOOSE is left alone.
She begins to weep as the Lights Fade to blackout.*)
(**LXQ.32**) (**FlyQ.4; LXQ.33**)

Scene Six

*The Edge of the Forest. (Gauze.) JACK, JILL, BILLY and the SQUIRE enter
from DL.*

BILLY: It's true . . .

JILL: It can't be . . .

BILLY: I'm telling you . . .

JACK: Don't blither, Billy . . .

SQUIRE: You're talking balderdash . . .

BILLY: You've got to believe me . . .

JILL: Mother Goose would *never* part with Priscilla . . .

SQUIRE: Not while there's cheese in Cheddar . . .

JACK: Not while there are olivers in Bath . . .

SQUIRE: Not while there's cake at Christmas . . .

BILLY: She sold her to this bloke.

JACK: What bloke?

MEPHISTO: (*Entering DL, pushing PRISCILLA along roughly*) Get a
move on, you feather-brained, foolish fowl . . .

BILLY: This bloke!

ALL: MEPHISTO!

(PRISCILLA is chained up around her wings with a great padlock at her neck.)

SQUIRE: Just a minute . . .

MEPHISTO: You talking to me, Squire?

JACK: Where are you going with Priscilla?

MEPHISTO: Pri-who-lla?

JACK: Our Goose.

MEPHISTO: *My* Goose.

JACK: Release her at once. Give me the key to this lock and let's get these chains off her . . .

MEPHISTO: But why? *(Embracing PRISCILLA, with a dagger at her back.)* She loves me . . .

ALL: *(Incredulous)* Loves *you*?

MEPHISTO: Don't you, little Goosey?

PRISCILLA: *(Terrified)* HONK . . . !

MEPHISTO: And she wants to come with me, don't you, Priscillakins? And . . . *(Producing the contract.)* She's mine! Take a gander at this, Squire?

(The SQUIRE takes the document.)

MEPHISTO: Does it or does it not make me the rightful owner of this Goose?

SQUIRE: *(Mumbling through the contract)* Heretofore . . . wheretofore . . . theretofore . . . signed, M Goose, Mother. Yes.

BILLY: It can't.

SQUIRE: I'm afraid it does.

JILL: We're her friends and we love her . . .

MEPHISTO: Very well then . . . One of you can come and keep her
              company. Let me see now . . . Ah yes . . . (*Taking JILL by
              the wrist.*) *You*, my dear. You'd like to come to my cave,
              wouldn't you? On a clear day, you can see the gasworks.

JACK: Enough of this. Document or no document, you're not
              taking Priscilla . . . Release her at once.

MEPHISTO: She's mine and she's coming with me . . .

JACK: You'll have to fight me first.

MEPHISTO: Oooo, I'm terrified.

JACK: Come on then . . .

MEPHISTO: Dratted boy . . . (*Taking a feather from his cloak with a
              POP.*) Ouch!
              Now with all the power of the mighty black feather
              I'll keep you at bay with some Mephisto Weather!

              (*Thunder. (SQ.15) Lightning. (LXQ.34) The GOODIES
              are blown, staggering across to DL. MEPHISTO exits DR
              roaring with laughter and dragging and kicking
              PRISCILLA as, clutching each other's hands, they begin to
              fight their way back.*)

JILL: (*Struggling against the wind*) What are we going to do?

JACK: We've got to get her back. We can't leave her in the
              clutches of that creep. But first we must find Mother and
              find out what this is all about. (*Fighting their way off DR.*)
              Mother . . . ! Mother . . . ?

              (*The Lights Fade to a mysterious glow.*) (*LXQ.35*)

MOTHER G: (*From the Stalls*) Hello . . . ? (*She is carrying a map.*) So
              this is Clapham Common. Or have I crept into the Crypt in
              King Street? No. (*Creeping up steps onto the stage.*)

(*LXQ.36; FSQ.9*)

MOTHER G: I seem to be in the right place. I'm so excited. It's like
              being on *Surprise Surprise*. But I do feel bad about letting
              Priscilla go like that. She was all I had in the whole wide
              world. But it was best, I think. I did right, didn't I?

AUDIENCE: NO.

MOTHER G: Oh yes I did!

AUDIENCE: OH NO YOU DIDN'T!

MOTHER G: Well I don't care. Hell hath no fury like a woman's corns.
So there. I want to be beautiful and I shall.

(Sound of tinkling water.) **(SQ.16)**

MOTHER G: But wait wait wait. What's that I hear?
A splash of water in my ear.
The tell-tale drips as droplets fall
'Tis here I must reveal my all.

I can hardly wait to plunge right in
To immerse myself right up to me chin
With one last duck me head will go
And I'll come back up all of a glow.

Music: THE STRIPPER **(LXQ.37; FSQ.9A)**

*(MOTHER GOOSE performs an elaborate strip routine –
cloak – hat – three skirts, three tops – a three-cupped
brassiere – (This is my sheepdog brassiere. It rounds 'em
up and points 'em in the right direction.) – a series of rip-
away (velcro) pants with signs including: BAN THE BUM.
L-PLATE. GROPE FOUR. DANGER – FALLOUT. UP THE
ROBINS. BLACK HANDS. THE END.)*

(LXQ.38; FSQ.9B)

MOTHER G: Now, It only remains for me to speak the spell . . .
(Reading.) "Turn round three times and speak this Motto:
Up your jumper and see the Grotto . . . "

(Lights fade up behind the Gauze **(LXQ.39)** *to reveal:)*

Scene Seven

*The Waterfall of Youth and Beauty. A glittering Waterfall cascades over
the entrance to a Cavern which is topped off with jewelled Fountains.
There are Water Nymphs draped about the rocks.*

MOTHER G: Well there it is . . . Viagra Falls. Look at that . . . The
Wonderful Waterfall of Youth and Beauty in the Grotto of
Gorgeousness . . . Isn't that nice . . . ?

So into the magic pool I go
For one of me favourite dips.
A packet of vim and a brillo pad
Should polish up me bits.

(FlyQ.5; LXQ.40; FSQ.9C)

(*Rhapsodic Music (Rachmaninov) as the NYMPHS dance.
During which MOTHER GOOSE disappears through the
waterfall and can be dimly seen (this is a double) bathing.
At the end of the dance, there is a Flash, C.* **(Pyro Q.12)**
*The NYMPHS draw back to present MOTHER GOOSE (now
bizarrely beautiful) as she enters through the waterfall.*)

(LXQ.41; FSQ.10)

(*JACK, JILL, the SQUIRE and BILLY rush in. Twin
FLASHES DR and DL* **(Pyro Q.13)** *bring on FAIRY
GOOSEFEATHER in despair DR and MEPHISTO
triumphant DL with PRISCILLA in chains.*)

JACK/JILL: OH MOTHER DEAR, WON'T YOU PLEASE STOP THESE
                                                    PRETENCES?
              WHAT CAN WE DO TO HELP YOU TO COME TO YOUR
                                                    SENSES?

FAIRY: AND NOW PRISCILLA IS LOST! (*Sobs.*)

GOODIES: WE PREFER ...

FAIRY: FOR THAT NASTY OLD CREEP ...

GOODIES: YOU AS YOU WERE ...

FAIRY: OUR PRISCILLA WILL KEEP ...

GOODIES: AND WE ALL CONCUR ...

FAIRY: SO ALL THAT REMAINS FOR ME IS TO SIT HERE AND
              WEEP!

GOODIES: ALAS, WE CAME TOO LATE ...

MEPHISTO: THE GOOSE BELONGS TO ME ...

GOODIES: TO SAVE HER FROM THIS FATE ...

MEPHISTO: AND NOW FOR THE SQUIRE'S DAUGHTER!

(LXQ.42)

(*MOTHER GOOSE has been standing on a concealed lift (ideally) and, during this final chorus, she will rise up majestically as her gown and train (on tripwires) fan out around her to make her look like a huge butterfly, filling the stage.*)

GOODIES/   OH, MOTHER DEAR, WHY CAN'T YOU SEE WHAT
FAIRY: YOU'RE DOING?

MEPHISTO: HA HA! PRISCILLA WILL BE THE BAIT!

GOODIES/   THERE'S MADNESS IN THIS COURSE YOU'RE PURSUING.
FAIRY:

MEPHISTO: HA HA! SHE'LL SOON BE IN MY GRASP!

(*The Music swells, MEPHISTO roars with maniacal laughter and ill-treats PRISCILLA. The GOODIES are in tormented attitudes of despair as the curtain falls.*)

(LXQ.43; FSQ.10A)

End of Act One.

ACT TWO

Scene One

In front of Pantomime Gauze.

Flash DL. (PyroQ.14) Crash of Thunder. (SQ.17; LXQ.44; FSQ.11)
MEPHISTO appears DL in a fury.

MEPHISTO: Curse and Drat it! Bother and blast!
I'm running out of patience fast.
While you've been out, three days have passed
And all unlucky.
The goose won't lay, though I threaten and rave –
And keep her chained up in my cave –
But not one ovoid of the gold I crave –
Not a single chuckie.

        (Flash DR.) (Pyro Q.15; LXQ.45; FSQ.12)

FAIRY: *(Leaping on)* Sucks jolly boo, you nasty nerd.

MEPHISTO: Ah! Curses! I've been overheard.

FAIRY: She won't lay for you, the wondrous bird –
She's a total brick.

MEPHISTO: I'll sort her out. You wait and see.
She only needs some company.
I'll persuade Mother Goose to come home with me.
That'll do the trick.
The silly woman will do as she's told
And *make* Priscilla lay eggs of gold
Or I'll *cook* the goose. She'll be casserolled
In an Irish stew!

        (A Crash of Thunder (SQ.18; LXQ.46; FSQ.11A) and he
        exits DL guffawing.)

FAIRY: I must act quickly and save Priscilla
From the clutches of that evil killer
The plot thickens, eh? Bit of a thriller?
Now what would Batman do?
Tell you what – while I have a ponder,
You can watch the dancing yonder
Where everything is bright and gay
Well, what d'you expect on the first of May?

(*Dissolve through gauze (**LXQ.47**) to:*)

Scene Two

The Village Green.

(*FlyQ.6; LXQ.48; FSQ.12A*)

ALL:
> Song: **THE FIRST OF MAY** *(JACK, JILL, the SQUIRE,*
> *BILLY and VILLAGERS)*
> (*During which, JILL is crowned as the May Queen*)
> DANCE AND SING ON THE VILLAGE GREEN.
> THIS FIRST OF MAY, WE GARLANDS BRING TO CROWN
> OUR QUEEN.
> TODAY'S THE DAY TO DANCE AND SING ON THE
> VILLAGE GREEN.
> OUR JUBILATION IS ENTRANCING,
> OUR REVELRY IS LIFE-ENHANCING,
> DISPLAYING OUR DELIGHT IN DANCING
> IS HOW WE TREASURE
> THIS GREAT PLEASURE
> IN OUR LEISURE
> ON THIS HOLIDAY.

(*LXQ.49*)

> (*MOTHER GOOSE enters from UL dressed as a ludicrous*
> *May Queen.*)

MOTHER G: Just a minute, just a minute . . .

BILLY: What do *you* want?

MOTHER G: What do *I* want?

SQUIRE: Yes. You're interrupting our festivities. It's the crowning
of the May Queen . . .

MOTHER G: May I enquire, Squire, how you can possibly have started
without me . . . ?

JACK: We've already crowned the May Queen – Jill. Look,
Mother. Was there ever a more beautiful Queen of the
May?

MOTHER G: But *I* was to be Queen of the May . . .

BILLY:	You look more like Match of the Day . . .
MOTHER G:	Now you listen to me. I was the best thing *before* sliced bread. As the richest, most ravishing and poshest person in these parts, I'll ask you to show some respect.
SQUIRE:	You'll get no respect from us, Mother Goose.
BILLY:	Not after what you been and gone and done.
VILL. A:	No. You give Priscilla away.
VILL. B:	We love Priscilla.
VILL. C:	But we don't love you.
VILL. D:	Not anymore. You're horrible . . .
VILL. E:	Nasty . . . And you look a mess . . .
MOTHER G:	No, you don't understand. I'm beautiful.
ALL:	You're NOT! (*They all turn on their heels and go.*)
MOTHER G:	(*To the AUDIENCE*) You think I'm beautiful, don't you?
AUDIENCE:	NO!
MOTHER G:	(*Wailing*) But I parted with Priscilla for this. If I'm not beautiful, I've been nasty for nothing. Surely *some*body thinks I'm beautiful . . .
MEPHISTO:	(*Singing – off DL*) When I'm calling you-hoo-hoo-hoo-hoo-hoo!
MOTHER G:	(*To a member of the AUDIENCE*) Was that you?
MEPHISTO:	(*Peering round the Proscenium*) Will you answer too-hoo-hoo-hoo-hoo-hoo-hoo . . . ?
MOTHER G:	It's the Wall's Ice Cream man.
MEPHISTO:	Oh, Mother Goose . . .
MOTHER G:	Don't you "Oh, Mother Goose" me. I've got a bone to pick with you. (*Tearfully.*) You told me I'd be beautiful and everybody says I'm not a *bit* beautiful and they used to

like me and now they *don't* and I've give away *Priscilla* and they all *hate* me and I'm very sad 'cos I've not got no friends and *nobody* loves me and . . .

MEPHISTO: Oh shut your mush, you blithering fool.

MOTHER G: What?

MEPHISTO: Oh hush, oh hush, my glittering jewel. You *are* beautiful. Of course you're beautiful . . .

MOTHER G: (*Indicating the AUDIENCE*) But they don't think so.

MEPHISTO: (*Glowering at the AUDIENCE*) Them? THEM? They should learn to belt up! They're only jealous.

MOTHER G: (*Coy*) Jealous? Of little me?

MEPHISTO: In your presence, even the loveliest must seem dowdy and dull. You must expect jealousy . . .

MOTHER G: Yes. I suppose I must. They're just cross 'cos they're not glitteringly gorgeous and cultured and sophisisticulated like as what I am.

MEPHISTO: There you are then, my proud beauty. Oh! Let me look at you. Oh the light – the line – the peerless perfection. A work of art like a Rodin or a Michelangelo.

MOTHER G: I know. I know. I even call my palace Lautrec.

MEPHISTO: Why?

MOTHER G: 'Cos it's got two loos.

MEPHISTO: (*Grabbing her*) Oh, Mother Goose, kiss me.

MOTHER G: I'm too shy!

MEPHISTO: I know. I've seen the coconuts. Kiss me.

MOTHER G: Why? Have you got shares in Mothercare?

MEPHISTO: Don't taunt me. Oh. I have a passion throbbing in my bosom.

MOTHER G: Oh let's have a look. I've lost one of me ferrets.

MEPHISTO: Be serious. With your beauty, the time is now ripe. My terms for marriage are very competitive. Are you prepared to ratify my proposals?

MOTHER G: Certainly. Place them on the table and pass me the mallet.

MEPHISTO: Oh you drive a hard bargain. I can feel a chill blowing through my arrangements.

MOTHER G: Would you like something to warm you up?

MEPHISTO: Yes please.

MOTHER G: I think I've got an extra strong mint in my drawers.

MEPHISTO: Let me take you out of all this. I want to escort you everywhere.

MOTHER G: Oooo, will you take me to the zoo?

MEPHISTO: If the zoo want you, let 'em come and get you. But wait, my angel. I like a woman with intellect. How many GCSE's did you get?

MOTHER G: Three. English, Spanish and rubbish.

MEPHISTO: Really? C'est magnifique, mon amour. Tres Gentil.

MOTHER G: Mercy buckets.

MEPHISTO: Come. Give me your hand. (*He kisses her palm.*) Allow me to kiss the backside.

MOTHER G: I beg your pardon.

(*Music intro:* HONEYSUCKLE AND THE BEE) (*LXQ.50; FSQ.13*)

MEPHISTO: Oh you're just a tease. You make me so jealous. Surely you realise that: (*Sings:*)
YOU ARE MY HONEY-HONEYSUCKLE, I AM THE BEE.

MOTHER G: I'D LIKE TO SIP THE HONEY SWEET FROM THOSE RED
LIPS, YOU SEE.

MEPHISTO: I LOVE YOU DEARLY DEARLY AND I WANT YOU TO
LOVE ME.

BOTH: YOU ARE MY HONEY-HONEYSUCKLE, I AM THE BEE.

(*LXQ.51; FSQ.13A*)

MEPHISTO: Marry me and live in my cave and Priscilla will lay me lots of
                 golden eggs . . .

MOTHER G: Eggs eggs eggs that's all you men ever think of . . . always
                 freeranging . . . always looking for a clutch . . . (*To the
                 AUDIENCE.*) Isn't that right, girls? And once you've
                 cracked it . . . the yolk's on us . . . after four minutes on the
                 timer, you scarper and leave us – scrambled . . .

MEPHISTO: Why else would I carry on this charade.

MOTHER G: Oh, omelettes . . .

MEPHISTO: Let's face it. You look horrible. Like an addled fleabag.
                 It's pitiful! But what care I? I have the Goose and it will lay
                 or I'll have it for my supper . . . Priscilla pie. (*He guffaws
                 and goes.*)

MOTHER G: Oh no. What am I to do? (*To the AUDIENCE.*) You do
                 think I look lovely, don't you?

AUDIENCE: NO.

MOTHER G: Well what do you think I look like? Well don't take a vote
                 on it. Godzilla? Who said that? You tyke. That trip to the
                 magic waterfall was exactly what I needed. See my skin is
                 so beautiful now. Taut, tense and tender – like a Buxted
                 chicken. I was right to give Priscilla away, wasn't I?

AUDIENCE: NO.

MOTHER G: Oh yes I was.

AUDIENCE: OH NO YOU WEREN'T.

MOTHER G: I don't believe you. Let's look in the mirror. The mirror
                 doesn't lie. (*She produces the mirror and looks into it. It
                 shatters into fragments again.*) Oh, boys and girls – Mums
                 and Dads – bus-pass holders – you're right – all of you. I
                 should never have let her go.

                 (*JACK and the others peer round the masking,
                 overhearing.*)

MOTHER G: D'you know, I've been so miserable since she went away. I don't know where to find her. I haven't got a friend in the world. Nobody loves me anymore.

(*JACK and the others creep up on her.*)

JACK: Oh Mother dear, don't be upset. You've made a terrible mistake. But if you can find it within yourself to say "sorry" . . .

MOTHER G: Sorry? Of course I'm sorry. I'm sorry, everybody. I'm sorry, boys and girls – I'm sorry, Jack and Jill. And I'm sorry, Priscilla . . . wherever you are . . . I'm sorry, I'm sorry.

JACK: Then we forgive you.

SQUIRE: Of course we do. Don't we, everybody?

ALL: Yes.

MOTHER G: Oh thank you. Thank you. You're so kind to me. But what about poor Priscilla. D'you think we should send out a search party to see if we can find her?

JACK: We'll do better. We'll send out a *rescue* party. We'll track Mephisto to his lair in the wicked woods and we'll rescue Priscilla and bring her home again.

JILL: Oh, Jack, you are brave.

JACK: I know. But I am the hero, after all.

MOTHER G: Oh you little tinker. Give me two minutes to slip into something sensible and we'll be off on the trail. Billy, come and pack the provisions for our journey . . .

(*BILLY and MOTHER GOOSE exit DR.*)

JACK: Now, who's with me?

JILL: I am.

SQUIRE: And I.

VILLAGERS: We all are.

(*Music: intro.*) (*LXQ.52; FSQ.14*)

JACK: Thank you, friends. But, if we're to take Mephisto by
surprise, only a few of us must go. A small but courageous
band.

               Song: **WE'RE ON THE ROAD** (*JACK, JILL, the SQUIRE
and VILLAGERS*)

JACK: WE MUST ALL BE BRAVE
FOR WHO CAN KNOW WHAT FATE AWAITS US IN THE
WICKED WOOD?
WE'LL DO OR DIE
BUT WE WILL NEVER FLY
NEVER FALTER IN OUR MISSION BUT WE'LL DO AS
HEROES SHOULD.
WE ARE READY –
STRONG AND STEADY –
WHEREVER WE HAVE TO ROAM.
WHATEVER MAY BEFALL,
WE'LL TRIUMPH OVER ALL
AND WE'LL BRING PRISCILLA HOME.

ALL: WE'RE ON THE ROAD TO ANYWHERE
WITH NEVER A HEARTACHE AND NEVER A CARE.
COMRADES ALL – BEST OF FRIENDS –
READY FOR ANYTHING THE GOOD LORD SENDS
ON THE ROAD TO ANYWHERE
WHERE EVERY MILESTONE SEEMS TO SAY
THAT, THROUGH ALL THE WEAR AND TEAR
THE ROAD TO ANYWHERE
WILL LEAD TO SOMEWHERE – SOMEDAY.

               (*They all march off as the lights blackout.*)   (*LXQ.53;
FSQ.14A*)

(*FlyQ.7; LXQ.54*)

                       Scene Three

The Edge of the Forest. (*Gauze.*)
(*FSQ.15*) *FAIRY GOOSEFEATHER marches on from DR.*

FAIRY: Oh, bliss! Oh joy! What jolly japes!
They're off to foil that jackanapes.
To seek and find Mephisto's cavy
Lest he cook the goose with Bisto gravy.
They face great danger. It'll scary be.
But they'll have the help of little fairy me.
I'll fly ahead to his witches coven

And break the timer on his oven.
But first make haste to find the venue
And keep Priscilla off the menu.

(LXQ.55; FSQ.15A)

> *(She marches off DR as the SQUIRE leads JACK, JILL,
> BILLY and MOTHER GOOSE, marching on, to drum
> accompaniment, singing the "Dad's Army" theme "Who do
> you think you are kidding, old Mephisto?" from DL.
> MOTHER GOOSE is dressed as a Girl Guide.)*

SQUIRE: Party . . . HALT!!

> *(They all pile up on one another and fall in a heap.)*

SQUIRE: No no no. This won't do at all. If we're going to mount a
surprise attack on Mephisto and rescue Priscilla, we must be
a disciplined fighting force. Firm jawed . . .

> *(They set their jaws.)*

SQUIRE: Narrow eyed . . .

> *(They narrow their eyes.)*

SQUIRE: Ferocious as lions . . .

> *(They all growl.)*

SQUIRE: Afraid of nothing . . .

> *(JILL sneezes. BILLY screams and jumps up into MOTHER
> GOOSE'S arms.)*

SQUIRE: Afraid of nothing, I said. Right now get back into line.

> *(They do.)*

SQUIRE: Atten – tion!

> *(They come to attention. BILLY is late.)*

SQUIRE: As you were. As you were. Stand at ease. Stand easy . . .

> *(BILLY falls to the floor.)*

SQUIRE: Not that easy. On your feet.

(*BILLY gets up.*)

SQUIRE: As you were, as you were.

(*BILLY falls down again.*)

BILLY: That's how I was.

SQUIRE: Atten-tion! Eyes front.

(*He prowls along the line, inspecting them.*)

SQUIRE: (*To JACK*) Don't you eyeball me. Bottom in, chest out. (*To JILL.*) Bottom in, chest out. (*BILLY is fascinated by JILL's chest – To BILLY.*) Bottom in, chest out. (*BILLY, still staring at JILL, contorts – To MOTHER GOOSE.*) Bottom in – out . . . chest . . . (*MOTHER GOOSE is swaying and contorting, trying to get it right.*) Oh, never mind! I hope you've all passed your medicals. Have you been x-rayed?

MOTHER G: No but I've been ultra violated.

SQUIRE: Right now. Get into line. From the right – number!

(*They all begin to dance wildly.*)

SQUIRE: What do you think you're doing?

BILLY: We thought you said "Rhumba".

SQUIRE: Pay attention, stupid! Again – from the right – number!

JACK: One.

JILL: Two.

BILLY: Three.

MOTHER G: Five.

SQUIRE: (*Pointing with his swagger stick at JACK'S boots*) Look at those boots. (*JACK looks down and the SQUIRE hits him on the head.*)

JACK: Ouch!

SQUIRE: (*To JILL*) Look at those boots. (*JILL looks down, he hits her on the head.*)

JILL: Ouch!

SQUIRE: (*To BILLY*) Look at those boots. (*BILLY looks down, he hits him on the head – there is no reaction.*) (*To MOTHER GOOSE.*) Look at those boots! (*She doesn't look.*)

BILLY: Ouch!

SQUIRE: (*To MOTHER GOOSE*) I said look at those boots. (*No reaction.*) LOOK AT THOSE BOOTS.

MOTHER G: You look. (*He looks down. She takes the stick and hits him on the head.*)

SQUIRE: Ouch!

MOTHER G: I'll have you know I'm a woman of peace.

SQUIRE: You'll be a woman in pieces if you don't do as you're told. Right now, we go to fight a fearful foe.

ALL: A fearful foe . . .

SQUIRE: He's mean.

ALL: He's mean . . .

SQUIRE: He's malicious.

ALL: He's malicious . . .

SQUIRE: He's Mephisto the Malevolent.

ALL: (*Clutching each other and trembling*) Ooooohhhh . . . !

SQUIRE: Now! Where are your arms?

ALL: (*Waving*) Yoo hooo . . .

SQUIRE: That's no use. You can't go into battle without arms. (*Calling off DL.*) We shall need arms. (*Four Mops are thrown on.*) Ah. The very latest technology. The Armalite forty-four callibre automatic . . . mop. Now then – men. We should move like poetry in motion.

BILLY:	I like poetry. I know a good one. "Mary Mary quite contrary . . ."
MOTHER G:	Pull up your socks. Your legs are hairy.
SQUIRE:	Don't be so stupid. Right, now pick up your mops. (*They scrabble about, picking up the Mops, getting tangled and managing to goose him several times.*) Right now. Squad!
ALL:	Yes!
SQUIRE:	Squa-a-a-a-ad!
ALL:	Ye-e-e-e-es?
SQUIRE:	Atten . . . SHUN!

(*They come to attention – BILLY is late.*)

SQUIRE:	Stand at . . EASE! Now stand like this. At ease with your arms.
BILLY:	(*Romantic, with the Mop*) Hello, baby. Did anyone ever tell you you had beautiful hair . . . ?
SQUIRE:	No, no, no! Hold your arms properly. Atten-shun! Legs together. (*BILLY is late.*) Now you slope arms like this. (*Demonstrating.*) One! Twooo, three . . . One! Twooo, three . . . One! . . . and throw it over your shoulder.
ALL:	One! Twoo three . . . One! Twooo three . . . One! And throw it over your shoulder. (*They throw their mops over their shoulders – onto the floor.*)
SQUIRE:	Don't be so stupid. Now pick 'em up. Pick em up pick 'em up pick em up. (*Chaos. Again, he gets goosed several times and gets stuck astride a mop.*) Right, now we'll do the present arms. Present arms!
ALL:	(*Giving him their mops*) "This is for you, as a token of . . ." "I'd like you to accept this on behalf . . ." (*Etc.*)
SQUIRE:	No no no. Now. Slope arms!
ALL:	ONE! . . . twoo, three . . . ONE! . . . twoo, three . . . ONE!

(*MOTHER GOOSE has her mop on the wrong (right) shoulder.*)

SQUIRE: Not there – (*Patting his left shoulder.*) There!

(*MOTHER GOOSE puts the Mop on his shoulder.*)

SQUIRE: Not there. Put it where he has his.

(*She puts the Mop on BILLY'S shoulder.*)

BILLY: Oh, ta, Mother Goose.

SQUIRE: (*Grabbing the Mop, raging, and putting it on her shoulder*) Put it there. Put it there. Put it there!

MOTHER G: Well why didn't you say? (*She suddenly produces a frying pan – which hangs on her belt – containing fried eggs and bacon – and shakes it about.*)

SQUIRE: What's that?

MOTHER G: Ready Brek.

SQUIRE: Now. If you were attacked, what steps would you take?

BILLY: Bloomin' great big ones.

SQUIRE: You couldn't defend anything. We'll need to exercise. Follow me. (*He runs on the spot.*) Knees well up. One two – one two – as if you're riding a bicycle.

(*They all do the same. MOTHER GOOSE stands still and leans on her mop.*)

SQUIRE: (*Running up to her*) What d'you think you're doing?

MOTHER G: I'm free-wheeling.

SQUIRE: Squad – atten . . .

(*They all raise their left legs.*)

SQUIRE: Wait for it . . . Shun! (*BILLY is still late.*) Qu-i-i-i-i-ick MARCH!

(*Muisc: Snare drum.*)

SQUIRE: Left wheel . . . (*BILLY goes right.*) Left wheel . . . (*MOTHER GOOSE about turns.*) Right wheel . . . About turn . . . Mark time . . . Quick march . . . etc. (*During all of which, he runs in amongst them as they march in all directions, managing to goose him or swing round and hit him on the head with their mops until, miraculously, they form up into a smart line.*)

BILLY: (*Like a US Marine marching platoon*) Who's the bravest in the land?

ALL: Who's the bravest in the land? (*Executing tricky mop twirls.*)

BILLY: Mother Goose's fearless band!

ALL: Mother Goose's fearless band! (*More Mop twirls.*)

BILLY: Stand aside we're on the track.

ALL: Stand aside we're on the track.

BILLY: We will bring Priscilla back!

ALL: We will bring Priscilla back!

                 (*Spectacular Mop business with snare drum accompaniment ending with a very smart shoulder arms, left turn and march off. MOTHER GOOSE hits the proscenium. Blackout.*)   (**LXQ.56**)

(**FlyQ.8; LXQ.57**)

Scene Four

A clearing in the Forest. (Seen through gauze.) Cackling WITCHES enter, dragging PRISCILLA in chains and prodding her with tridents. MEPHISTO enters UC sharpening a carving knife.

MEPHISTO: Boil up the cauldron . . . Sharpen the knives . . . Prepare the Paxo! Cook the Goose . . . Priscilla pie! Delicious! Give her two hours at regulo six and call me when she's done to a crisp . . . Ha ha ha . . .

                 (*He exits UC, cackling maniacally. FAIRY GOOSEFEATHER appears from R. The WITCHES scream. She waves her wand at them and they freeze, paralysed.*

She waves her wand at PRISCILLA'S chains and they fall to the floor.)

FAIRY: Come on, Priscilla, you're safe with me.
I told you all would end up happilee!

(She releases the WITCHES, who scuttle off L, screaming and leads PRISCILLA off R. The Gauze flies out (Fly Q.9; LXQ.58) as The GOODIES enter UC.)

JACK: *(Leading the way with drawn sword)* They've been here, I'm sure of it . . .

JILL: *(Pointing to R)* Look . . .

SQUIRE: What?

JILL: *(Picking it up)* One of Priscilla's feathers . . .

MOTHER G: Oh, poor Priscilla, what have they done to you?

BILLY: Which way did they go?

JACK: That's the point. We'll have to split up. *(Pointing off L.)* Squire, you go down the gully into the Gorge. *(Leading JILL towards R.)* Jill and I will take the high path up through the woods.

SQUIRE: *(Going – nervously)* Willco.

MOTHER G: And what shall we do?

JACK: Stay near in case they return. You'll need to conceal yourselves so that you can leap out and take them by surprise. Come on, Jill. Stick close to me and don't make a sound. *(They exit R.)*

(JILL shrieks, off.)

MOTHER G: *(Calling after them)* Stop that, Jack. Jack's right though, Billy, we must catch him unaware . . .

BILLY: Why do we want to catch him in his underwear?

MOTHER G: Unawares. If only we could disguise ourselves . . .

BILLY: I can do bird impersonations.

MOTHER G: What d'you do? Whistle?

BILLY: No. I eat worms.

MOTHER G: (*Hitting him*) Silly boy. Now get along with you. (*They exit L. Blackout.*) (***LXQ.59; FlyQ.10***)

(***LXQ.60***)

Scene Five

The edge of the Forest. (*Gauze.*) *FAIRY GOOSEFEATHER enters DR, comforting PRISCILLA.*

FAIRY: Come along, Priscilla. Dry your tears, you're safe now . . .

PRISCILLA: HONK!

FAIRY: Yes, I know you're terribly hurt by Mother Goose's selfishness but I shall send you off to Gooseland . . .

PRISCILLA: HONK?

FAIRY: You'll be happy there. I'll give you a letter of introduction to King Gander and he'll look after you – just as he looks after all the little orphan goslings . . .

     (*They exit DL as JACK and JILL enter DR.*)

(***LXQ.61; SQ.19***)

JACK: Ssshh!

     (*JILL trips. There is a "Ding-Dong" in the orchestra pit.*)

JACK: What was that?

JILL: I tripped over a bluebell.

JACK: Ssshh!

JILL: (*To the* (*imaginary*) *Bluebell*) Sssh! I wish Carpenter was here.

JACK: Who's Carpenter?

JILL: My dog.

JACK: Why do you call him Carpenter?

JILL: He's always doing little jobs about the house.

JACK: I'm glad I've got you beside me, Jill. I know I can depend on you.

JILL: Oh yes, Jack. I'm like a potato.

JACK: Why a potato?

JILL: I'm always there when the chips are down.

(There is a rustling off DL.)

JACK: What was that?

JILL: What?

(The rustling is repeated.)

JACK: That. In those bushes. Something stirred. Hello?

VOICE: Hello?

JACK: There's somebody there.

JILL: No. It's only an echo.

JACK: Echo?

JILL: Listen. Hello?

VOICE: Hello?

JILL: I know where . . .

VOICE: I know where . . .

JILL: You can get . . .

VOICE: You can get . . .

JILL: A bottle of whisky . . .

VOICE: A bottle of whicky . . .

JILL: For twenty p . . .

SQUIRE: *(Leaping on)* Where?

JILL: I might have known.

JACK: What were you doing in those bushes, Squire?

SQUIRE: I was trying to make myself invisible.

JACK: And you were partly successful.

SQUIRE: How's that?

JACK: You're not all there.

SQUIRE: Charming. But enough of this. (*Crossing to R.*) I'm going home.

JACK: But Mephisto . . .

SQUIRE: I left the cooker on . . .

JACK: But . . .

SQUIRE: I forgot to put the cat out . . .

JILL: But, Daddy . . .

SQUIRE: (*Tangoing off DR*) It's time for my tango class . . .

JILL: Poor Daddy, he never was very brave.

JACK: But you're not afraid of anything.

JILL: Not while we're . . . side by side . . .

               (*Music: intro.*)

JACK: Arm in arm . . .

JILL: Hand in hand . . .

(*FSQ.16; LXQ.62*)

> **Song: ARM IN ARM** (*JACK and JILL*)
> SIDE BY SIDE, YOU AND I,
> A PERFECT TEAM, YOU CAN'T DENY.
> YES, SIDE BY SIDE, WE'LL KEEP ON TRAVELLING ON.
> ARM IN ARM, DAY BY DAY,
> THOUGH THE SUN MAY LOSE IT'S WAY.
> JUST ARM IN ARM, WE'LL KEEP ON TRAVELLING ON.
> HERE WITHIN THIS SPOOKY OLD WOOD,
> TROUBLED BY STORMY WEATHER,
> I BELIEVE OUR PROSPECTS ARE GOOD
> AS LONG AS WE STICK TOGETHER.
> HAND IN HAND, WE INTEND
> TO BATTLE ON 'TIL JOURNEY'S END.

YES, HAND IN HAND, WE'LL KEEP ON TRAVELLING ON.

(LXQ.63; FSQ.16A)

JILL: (*Whispering*) Sshh!

(*MOTHER GOOSE backs on from DL, wittering with fear. They don't see her.*)

JACK: (*Whispers*) What was that?

(*BILLY, also wittering, backs on from DR.*)

JILL: (*Whispers*) And that. This wood's so dark and eerie and full of horrible things . . .

ALL: (*Colliding*) AAAHHH!

BILLY: I just saw a pair of horrible green eyes over there . . .

(*MEPHISTO peers round the proscenium DL, accompanied by some of his WITCHES.*)

MOTHER G: And I saw a pair of horrible red eyes over there.

(*More WITCHES peer round the proscenium DR. MEPHISTO is tiptoeing behind the GOODIES.*)

JILL: It's as if the very trees were alive . . .

BILLY: We're surrounded . . .

JACK: Then, if we're surrounded, we'll have to fight our way out.

MEPHISTO: (*Seizing JILL*) Too late. You're no match for my magical mates. Come along, girlie, my cavern awaits . . . (*He exits, DR, dragging JILL.*)

JACK: (*Fighting his way through the WITCHES' tridents to follow*) Unhand her, you brute . . . Be brave, Jill . . . I'm coming . . .

(*The WITCHES spin MOTHER GOOSE and BILLY round until they are dizzy – so that they end up fighting each other.*)

MOTHER G: Take that and that and that and that! (*Recognising him.*) Oh! Sorry Billy!

BILLY: That's alright. (*Hits her.*)

                (*The gauze flies out* (**FLY Q.11**) *to reveal:*)   (**LQ.64**)

                            Scene Six

*The Clearing. MEPHISTO is dragging JILL in chains. The WITCHES form
a ring of tridents around them. JACK rushes on and carves his way
through the WITCHES who run off screaming.*

JACK: Unhand her, Mephisto . . .

MEPHISTO: Curses. (*Backing away DC.*) Foolish youth. (*Pulling a
                Black Feather from his cloak.*) Ouch! But you can't
                overcome the power of . . . the black feather!

                (*BILLY enters from R with the huge Club.*)

MEPHISTO: Oh mighty black feather with power to blight . . .

BILLY: Oh – look up there!

MEPHISTO: Where?

BILLY: And so – goodnight!

                (*BILLY clunks MEPHISTO on the head. The Black Feather
                falls into the orchestra pit, causing awful dischords.*)

MEPHISTO: (*Staggering*) Oh drat! Oh bum! Oh fiddlededee!
                But you haven't seen the last of me. (*He rushes off DL with
                a Clap of Thunder.*) (**SQ.20**)

                (*MOTHER GOOSE totters on from R, gasping for breath.
                JACK strikes the chains with his sword. They fall to the
                ground, releasing JILL who rushes into his arms.*)

JILL: My hero!

MOTHER G: Stop that, stop that! Where's Priscilla?

BILLY: He's still got her . . .

JACK: He must still have her hidden away somewhere.

MOTHER G: So we're back where we were. Who knows what he might
                do to her.

(A FLASH DR and FAIRY GOOSEFEATHER appears.)

FAIRY: Fear not. I have rescued Priscilla from Mephisto's malice
And sent her to safety in King Gander's Palace.
In that fleecy land of geese above
She'll find a welcome – and peace and love.

MOTHER G: But *we* love her.

FAIRY: A pity you didn't show it.
Priscilla couldn't stay here – even when free.
Her heart was broken by your cruelty.

BILLY: But who are you?

FAIRY: Fairy Goosefeather. Patron fairy of all goslings and geese.

MOTHER G: And has she really flown away from me?

FAIRY: She took off from Fairford at three twenty-nine.

(PRISCILLA (a puppet) flies upwards at an angle (on a guide wire) across the back, trailing a banner saying "GOODBYE FOR EVER".) (FlyQ.12)

FAIRY: There she goes. Wave goodbye. For the very last time.

MOTHER G: Oh no. Oh no. I can't bear it.

JACK: How can we get her back?

FAIRY: She doesn't *want* to come back.

MOTHER G: But if only we could ask her . . . Beg her . . .

FAIRY: I suppose you *could* go to Gooseland and plead with King Gander – and ask Priscilla to forgive you.

MOTHER G: Oh yes. Let's do that. *(Flapping her arms.)* Come on, everybody . . .

BILLY: *(Flapping his arms)* It's not a bit of blooming use.

JILL: We've got no wings . . .

MOTHER G: Or propellor things . . .

JACK: We'll never see our goose . . .

FAIRY: Fret not, you'll be in Gooseland soon –

               (*The FAIRY casts a complicated spell and points off L.*)

FAIRY: I'll conjure you a hot-air balloon.
               You'll be there by tea this afternoon
               I should have thought.

MOTHER G: This way!

               (*The GOODIES rush off L.*)

FAIRY: (*Calling after*) Board the basket and ride the breeze.
               Straight on up at ninety degrees.
               Watch out for those poplar trees
               And don't get caught

               (*The Balloon (Cut-out) flies across the sky* (**FlyQ.13**) *with puppet JACK, JILL, BILLY and MOTHER GOOSE waving.*)

FAIRY: I'll fly ahead and let them know
               You're on your way up from below
               See you up there. Mind how you go.
               (*Taking off and hovering.*) It's my favourite sport. (*She flies off R.*)

               (*Music: Transformation to:*) (**LXQ.65; FlyQ.14**)

(**LXQ.66**)

Scene Seven

The Palace of King Gander. A flock of GOSLINGS dance a "Gooselake Ballet" as part of the transformation. KING GANDER enters with FAIRY GOOSEFEATHER and PRISCILLA during this and ascends his throne UC.

(**LXQ.67**)

KING G: Charming, my goslings. What do you think, Priscilla?

               (*PRISCILLA nods sadly.*)

FAIRY: Oh golly. You're not at all happy here, are you?

               (*PRISCILLA nods sadly.*)

KING G: You know, I believe it's because you miss all your friends
                back home. Is it?

PRISCILLA: HONK.

FAIRY: You miss Mother Goose, do you?

PRISCILLA: (*Shakes her head "No" – then nods "Yes"*) HONK.

                (*Fanfare.*)

GOSLING: (*Fluttering on from L*) King Gander . . . Strange creatures at
                the portals.

GOSLING: (*Joining her*) Without feathers. They must be mortals.

KING G: Mortals in the Land of Geese?
                When will they learn to leave us in peace?
                Bring them before me.

                (*The GOSLINGS push and drive MOTHER GOOSE, JACK,
                JILL and BILLY on from R.*)

MOTHER G: What a strange and wonderful place. Hello, little goslings!

GOSLINGS: HISS.

MOTHER G: Well please yourselves. (*Seeing PRISCILLA.*) Oh . . .
                Priscilla! Priscilla, my darling bird . . .

                (*She tries to rush to PRISCILLA but the GOSLINGS hold
                her back and PRISCILLA hides her head under her wing.*)

KING G: One moment. Is this the Mother Goose of whom I have
                heard so many evil things?

FAIRY: It is, your Majesty. But I'm sure she's sorry for what she
                did.

MOTHER G: Oh I am. I am, your Gandership . . .

KING G: (*Sternly*) Silence . . .

FAIRY: I brought her here, your Majesty, so that they could be
                reconciled.

KING G: I always knew you were more than the average fairy.

FAIRY:	Corks, ta, Thing is though, Gander, that Priscilla is jolly sad without Mother Goose. And Mother Goose is jolly, *jolly* sad without Priscilla. She knows she did wrong but she doesn't know what to say to Priscilla.
KING G:	Mother Goose – step forward.
MOTHER G:	(*Humbly*) Yes, your Kingsdown?
KING G:	You have been a bad woman. You sent away your best friend
MOTHER G:	I know but I only . . .
KING G:	Silence. Don't interrupt. You betrayed her friendship, her trust, and took away the innocence of a poor goose.
MOTHER G:	I know, but I only . . .
KING G:	Will you be quiet? I won't have these interruptions.
MOTHER G:	Sorry, your Kingship.
KING G:	Because of these things, we commit you to . . . trial by goose.
JACK/JILL: BILLY:	Trial!

(*There is an instant Lighting Change (**LXQ.68**) to sinister shadows with a harsh spot on MOTHER GOOSE.*)

KING G:	Mother Goose, you are charged with that you willfully and knowingly and with malice of forethought abandoned your best friend.
GOSLINGS:	HISS.
KING G:	You were thinking only of yourself.
GOSLINGS:	HISS.
KING G:	You didn't care what became of her. You were selfish.
MOTHER G:	I know it was wrong, your Kingship. But I wanted so much to be beautiful. So much so that I didn't care about anyone or anything.

KING G: You mean that your vanity meant more to you than your best friend?

MOTHER G: I realise now that it was wrong but, at the time . . . Oh . . . Please, Priscilla, can you ever forgive me? Oh please, Mr King, let me have my darling Priscilla back.

KING G: I'm afraid you've got it all wrong. She's not *your* Priscilla, Mother Goose. A Goose isn't just for Christmas, you know. She's come here to live in Gooseland thanks to Fairy Goosefeather.

            (*FAIRY GOOSEFEATHER bows and the GOSLINGS flap and hiss.*)

MOTHER G: You see . . . (*Moving sadly DR.*) I just keep thinking of myself. I'm sure she'll want to stay here. She wouldn't want to come back with me now . . . Would you, Priscilla? Not now you could live here for ever. It's such fun here – for a Goose. Living in a palace. And I shall be leaving my palace and moving back into my damp and draughty windmill like before. I mean, why would you want to come back to our shabby little home and live with ugly old me?

            (*PRISCILLA peeps out from under her wing.*)

MOTHER G: Priscilla . . . *will* you come home with me? I don't want to be rich . . .

            (*PRISCILLA takes a step towards her.*)

MOTHER G: I don't want to be beautiful . . .

            (*PRISCILLA takes another step.*)

MOTHER G: I just want to be happy. And *none* of us can be happy if you aren't with us.

            (*PRISCILLA – another step.*)

MOTHER G: Will you come back with me? Please?

            (*PRISCILLA slips her wingtip into MOTHER GOOSE'S hand.*)

JACK/JILL: HURRAY!
BILLY:

            (*The Lights return to normal.*) (**LXQ.69**)

KING G: I think she has already forgiven you Mother Goose.
            Priscilla – Do you really want to go home with Mother
            Goose?

PRISCILLA: NODS "YES", HONKS.

KING G: Then the trial is over. Mother Goose, you're free to go.
            And take Priscilla with you. I think this calls for a
            celebration. Goslings . . . Won't you sing and dance for
            Priscilla?

(*LXQ.70; FSQ.17*)

            Song: **THAT'S MY WEAKNESS NOW** (MOTHER GOOSE,
            PRISCILLA, GOSLINGS)

MOTHER G: LOVE, LOVE, LOVE, LOVE –
            ISN'T IT FINE TO SEE?
            PRISCILLA'S BACK WITH ME –
            SHE'S COMING HOME WITH ME.
            LOVE, LOVE, LOVE, LOVE –
            ISN'T IT PLAIN TO SEE?
            I'VE JUST HAD A CHANGE OF PLAN –
            WHAT CAN IT BE?

ALL: SHE'S GOT EYES OF BLUE, I NEVER CARED FOR EYES
                                                      OF BLUE
            BUT SHE'S GOT EYES OF BLUE AND THAT'S MY
                                               WEAKNESS NOW.
            SHE'S GOT FLIPPY-FLOPPY FEET, I NEVER CARED FOR
                                            FLIPPY-FLOPPY FEET
            BUT SHE'S GOT FLIPPY-FLOPPY FEET AND THAT'S MY
                                               WEAKNESS NOW.
            OH MY! OH ME!
            I NEVER HEARD OF SUCH A BIRD AS SHE.
            SHE LAYS EGGS OF GOLD, I NEVER CARED FOR EGGS OF
                                                          GOLD
            BUT SHE LAYS EGGS OF GOLD AND THAT'S MY
                                               WEAKNESS NOW.

            (*They burst into an energetic Tap Routine – in line like
            Tiller Girls. The line taps off stage L and back on again,
            having been joined by MEPHISTO wearing a Gosling tutu
            and feathery hat. As the dance continues, he moves
            stealthily up the line until he is level with PRISCILLA.*)

(*LXQ.71; FSQ.17A*)

MEPHISTO: (*Throwing off his disguise and grabbing PRISCILLA, a dagger at her throat*) Not so fast, you feathered and
                                          featherless fools.
             You seem to forget that Mephisto rules.
             Keep back, I say, I'm a vicious killer
             Alive or dead, I'll take Priscilla.

KING G: But this is Gooseland – my domain.

MEPHISTO: Oh shut your beak. The Goose is mine again.

JACK: (*Drawing his sword*) Not so fast, Mephisto, you evil blight.
             Let her go, coward. Turn and fight.

MEPHISTO: (*Backing away, dragging PRISCILLA*) One false move and
             the Goose gets hers . . .

             (*PRISCILLA stamps on his foot.*)

MEPHISTO: Aaah!

JACK: Quick, Priscilla, out of harm's way.
             Now, Mephisto – what do you say . . . ?

MEPHISTO: (*Drawing his sword*) Alright, alright! Don't get shirty.
             But watch yourself, 'cos I fight dirty!

             (*They fight. Sure enough, MEPHISTO fights dirty and
             nearly overcomes JACK. But JACK rallies, beats away
             MEPHISTO'S sword and has him at his mercy.*)

KING G: Now. What are we to do with you, evil birdman?
             Prison? Probation? No wait – I've a third plan.
             You're dressed as a gosling – though your disguise is but
                                                             cursory.
             Then you shall live as a gosling – in the gosling nursery.
             There to play 'til you've served your time
             Learning Gosling nursery rhymes.

             (*GOSLINGS lead away MEPHISTO off R, mumbling
             "Goosey Goosey Gander".*)

             (*Music: intro.*)

JACK: You see, friends, there's nothing we can't do – if we stick
             together.

(*LXQ.72; FSQ.18*)

ALL:

Song: ARM IN ARM (*Reprise*) (*FULL CAST*)
SIDE BY SIDE – WHAT A DAY –
A PERFECT TEAM IN EVERY WAY.
OUR HEARTS ARE LIGHT
NOW WE ARE TRAVELLING HOME.
ARM IN ARM –
WHAT A DAY –
NOW IT'S ROSES ALL THE WAY.
OUR HEARTS ARE LIGHT
NOW WE ARE TRAVELLING HOME.

(*MEPHISTO is pushed across in a pram by two GOSLINGS.
He wears a baby bonnet and is sucking a huge dummy.*)

OLD MEPHISTO'S NOW GOT HIS DUE
FOR CONDUCT BOTH GRIM AND GORY.
THANKS TO JACK AND PRISCILLA, TOO
EVERYTHING'S HUNKY-DORY.

ARM IN ARM –
RIDING HIGH –
LIFE IS GREAT WE CAN'T DENY.
OUR HEARTS ARE LIGHT NOW WE ARE TRAVELLING
HOME.

(*Blackout.*)   **(*LXQ.73; FSQ.18A; FlyQ.15*)**

(LXQ.74)

Scene Eight

Lover's Lane.

Songsheet.
GOOSE GOOSE GOOSE GOOSE GOOSEY,
LAY A LITTLE EGG FOR ME.
GOOSE, GOOSE GOOSE GOOSE GOOSEY –
I WANT ONE FOR MY TEA.
I HAVEN'T HAD AN EGG SINCE EASTER
AND NOW IT'S HALF PAST THREE.
SO –
GOOSE GOOSE GOOSE GOOSEY,
LAY A LITTLE EGG FOR ME!

(*LXQ.75; FSQ.19; FlyQ.16*)

Scene Nine

Walkdown.

FINALE (*FULL CAST*)

ALL: HAPPY AT LAST,
DANGER HAS PASSED,
WELCOME TO MERRIMENT AND LAUGHTER.
AFTER THIS MESS
YOU ALL CAN GUESS,
WE SHALL LIVE HAPPY EVER AFTER.
HAPPY, HAPPY, HAPPY,
WE'LL LIVE HAPPY EVER AFTER.
ALWAYS BE WISE AND YOU WILL RECALL,
PRIDE OFTEN COMES BEFORE A FALL.
BUT AS OUR STORY NOW CONTENDS
IT'S NEVER TOO LATE TO MAKE AMENDS.

MOTHER G: I'VE MADE A START
AND TAKEN HEART,
NOW THAT PRISCILLA IS RETURNING.
ALL WILL BE WELL
TRUTH TO TELL,

ALL: AND WE MAY STILL GO ON LEARNING.
HAPPY, HAPPY, HAPPY, WE'LL LIVE HAPPY EVER AFTER.
WE HOPE YOU ALL ENJOYED THE SHOW.
TIME HAS COME FOR US TO GO.
BUT WE'LL BE WAITING, HAVE NO FEAR,
SO COME AND SEE US ALL NEXT YEAR.

(LXQ.76; FSQ.19A)

(*Curtain. The End.*)

Props Plot

ACT ONE

Scene One – PANTOMIME GAUZE.

Wand for FAIRY BLODWEN.
Black Feather for MEPHISTO – he produces a whole series of these by pulling them out of his cloak and wincing with pain each time as if he's being plucked. Perhaps his cloak is made entirely of black feathers?

Scene Two – VILLAGE GREEN. MOTHER GOOSE'S WINDMILL.

The Windmill: This is a Cut-out flat UC with the cut-out Sails driven by a handle on the back. There is strategically placed velcro on one of the sails to attach the Dummy BILLY and he can either be yanked off by a line attached to him or actually snatched off as he goes past if the sightline allows.

Policeman's Helmet, Cape and Truncheon for BILLY.
Black Feather in SQUIRE'S Hat.

The Goosemobile – this is an optional device to give MOTHER GOOSE a good entrance. Ideally, it's a gooselike body which she wears on shoulder straps with a long flexible neck and a head which MOTHER GOOSE controls on stiff reins enabling her to "goose" people. There are dummy legs at the sides to give the impression that she is riding it and her own legs with yellow stripy tights and goose-feet over her own boots complete the effect. She has to be able to get out of it quickly and hand it to the VILLAGERS to take off.

Water Pistol for MOTHER GOOSE.
Super-Soaker (pump-action water gun) Off DL.
Full-sized Fireman's Hose (Nozzle and short length of hose) Off DL.
Basket of mini chocolate eggs (for give-away) Off DL.
Life-sized (soft, stuffed) Dummy of BILLY seen from the back – Off UC to be attached to the Windmill as described above.

Scene Three – INTERIOR OF MOTHER GOOSE'S COTTAGE.

There is a rocking chair LC, a table C with a cloth to the floor. This cloth is attached to a false plywood top which can be removed as a piece to show the conveyor belt. This is apparently MOTHER GOOSE'S corset running over a roller at each end – the roller at the onstage end is driven by a handle which is inserted when required. A high cupboard R and various shelves for the "Vase, Vaze or Vawse" props. There are stairs leading up to PRISCILLA'S basket over the cupboard. There is a Sheilamaid hanging from a ceiling beam RC and a little wooden chandelier hanging C.

Letter for PRISCILLA.
Laundry Basket for BILLY.
Note book and pencil for BILLY.

The following are placed on shelves or in cupboards for the convenience of the routine:

Vase.
Kettle.
Teapot (with the spout broken off).
Hand brush.
Candle in (Wee Willy Winkie-type) Candlestick.
Rubber Hot Water Bottle.
Child's Potty.
China Ornament – as ornate as possible.
Large Plastic Garden Gnome (the largest possible).
Pair of brightly coloured Sheets.
Huge pair of Fluffy Slippers.
Pair of very loud, checked Trousers.

Eggs   (Already in PRISCILLA):
One naturally coloured medium-sized (about 7") Egg.
One Golden Egg of the same size.
One large (about 12") Golden Egg.

She will probably need to visit the US trap for a reload to carry:
One huge (about 18") Golden Egg.
Two small (about 5") Golden Eggs.

Corset – concealed under the table cloth for MOTHER GOOSE to (apparently) take it off and rig it as a conveyor belt.
Handle (to drive the conveyor) hidden under the Table.

PRISCILLA, up on her nest, then (apparently) lays a stream of the small-sized Golden Eggs which are, in fact, fed to her through a convenient trap in the flat. She then drops them through the hole in the nest to roll down the Sheilamaid and along the conveyor belt, dropping off the onstage end to roll down a length of Guttering into a Ladle held by BILLY. He then flicks them high in the air across the stage to be caught by VILLAGERS, packed into baskets and taken off stage R to be passed to PRISCILLA again ad infinitum. We found we needed 40 of these eggs to keep up a steady flow through the song. There can also be an Easter Egg among them and MOTHER GOOSE can have a joke Fried Egg hidden. The last Egg should be special in some way. Ours had a spring-loaded top which flicked up to reveal a fluffy yellow chick on a spring – "Aaaw!".

Scene Four – FRONT CLOTH (LOVERS' LANE).

Black Feather (removable) in the SQUIRE'S Hat.

Huge Club concealed under MEPHISTO'S Cloak. He is hit on the head by this so it needs to be gigantic and ferocious-looking but soft (foam with a cane stiffening?)

Scene Five – MOTHER GOOSE'S PALACE OF GOLD.

A balcony UC with arches leading to it R and L also staircases leading down from it R and L to stage level. In front of the balcony C stands the "Tiddlypot". This can be simply a Pot on its side, capable of pouring liquid *or* it can be something like a tea-urn *OR*, ideally, it can be a Greek-type statue bearing a tilted urn on its shoulder and a basket worn on a sling at the hip. The figure wears a loincloth and is operated by a person sitting masked behind it. If the statue is used, then the operators arm can be its arm. The operator has a selection of old (clean) washing-up liquid containers filled with suitably coloured liquid. These can then be squeezed down whatever pipework is involved and into the glass held by MOTHER GOOSE – or squirted directly into BILLY'S eye. If the statue idea is used, this last can be considerably ruder. There is also a Slice of Lemon, a Cube of Ice (perspex) and a Cocktail Umbrella.

There is a table R with bowls of cakes, sandwiches and exotic fruit and a table L with bottles of wine, glasses and a soda syphon. All of the bowls and plates should be on plywood stands raised an inch above the table top on rods. This is so that the Tablecloth can be slit to fit around the rods and MOTHER GOOSE can (apparently) whip the cloth off to use in the Tango while leaving all the food intact. Some of the Fruit can be used to form a Head-dress and Ear-rings for MOTHER GOOSE in the same routine. Bananas are used as Bull's horns by the SQUIRE.

Cocktail Glasses (plastic) by the Tiddly Pot.
Feather Dusters, Cloths, Brooms, etc, for the FOOTMEN and
    PARLOURMAIDS.
Large Handbag for MOTHER GOOSE. This contains a Funnel and a
    length of Hose.
Hot Water Bottle concealed in BILLY'S trousers.
Handmirror concealed but easily accessible by the Tiddly Pot. This
    needs to (apparently) shatter and the face is composed of a
    spiky jig-saw of thin silvered plywood loosely attached by
    string to the frame so that, when MOTHER GOOSE jumps, it
    flies into fragments.
Contract for MEPHISTO. This is a very long (toilet paper width) piece
    of cloth covered with copious writing, rolled round a dowel so
    that he can let it unroll in one beat.
Ornate Certificate for MEPHISTO (Ticket to the Grotto).

Scene Six – THE EDGE OF THE FOREST.

Network of Chains (plastic) and huge Padlock – binding PRISCILLA.
Dagger for MEPHISTO.

Map for MOTHER GOOSE.

THE STRIP: MOTHER GOOSE wears a huge coat (and might have two or three others under it before getting down to the first dress – or blouse and skirt – and several of those before reaching underwear). Then there is a huge brassiere (possibly with three cups) "I call this my sheepdog brassiere – it rounds 'em up and points 'em in the right direction", a corset (which can be played as an accordion) and then a series of rip-off knickers (velcroed legs) each pair of which has a caption: "Ban the Bum", "Not Wanted on Voyage", "L" plates, references to local football clubs, local civic campaigns, etc, ending in a grotesque sort of swim suit.

ACT TWO

Scene Two – THE VILLAGE GREEN.

May Queen Crown for JILL.
Garlands for VILLAGERS, BILLY and the SQUIRE.
Sword in scabbard on belt for JACK.

Scene Three – THE EDGE OF THE FOREST (GAUZE).

Officer's Swaggerstick for the SQUIRE.
Small Frying Pan hanging from MOTHER GOOSE'S Belt with Eggs and
    Bacon glued into it.
Four ordinary Domestic Mops.

Scene Four – A CLEARING IN THE FOREST.

Tridents for the WITCHES.
Carving Knife and Sharpener for MEPHISTO.
One of PRISCILLA'S Feathers on floor.

Scene Five – THE EDGE OF THE FOREST.

Chains (plastic) for MEPHISTO – to bind JILL.

PRISCILLA Puppet – this can be a cut-out (though it's nice if the wings flap) and is pulled up a thin wire stretched diagonally between the floor and whichever fly gallery or other high fixing point is convenient. It is pulled up by a fishing line and runs on curtain rings together with its trailing Banner.

BALLOON – This is also a cut-out and can work on the same principle or, if large, can be tracked on a tab-track and flown at the same time to achieve the diagonal. Ideally, the figures are waving as they go – battery powered by one of those excellent model-maker's electric motors.

Scene Seven – THE PALACE OF KING GANDER.

Sword for MEPHISTO – at least half hidden under his tu-tu.
Dagger for MEPHISTO.
Huge Baby's Dummy for MEPHISTO.
Pram – in which MEPHISTO is pushed across.

Lighting Plot

ACT ONE

Cue	Detail
1	Very sinister green area for MEPHISTO DL.
2	Pretty pink area for FAIRY GOOSEFEATHER DR.
3	Lose MEPHISTO light DL.
4	Crossfade to the VILLAGE GREEN seen through the Panto Gauze.
5	(*Gauze out*) VILLAGE GREEN – bright, sunny day for Opening Number.
6	Build for Chorus.
7	Build for Final Chorus.
8	Romantic for JACK and JILL Duet.
9	Return to state of LXQ7.
10	Build for MOTHER GOOSE'S Entrance.
11	Very colourful – possible Disco throb – for MOTHER GOOSE song.
12	Interior of MOTHER GOOSE'S COTTAGE.
13	Very dramatic "freeze" – inc. MEPHISTO DL.
14	Add FAIRY DR.
15	Lose MEPHISTO Light.
16	"Magic" LIGHT.
17	State of LXQ12.
18	Pulsing, rhythmic light for EGG-LAYING MACHINE.
19	Snap B.O.
20	LOVERS' LANE – Nasty day.
21	LOVER'S LANE – Lovely day Stage Right.
22	Lose lovely day – sinister (but comedy) Acting Light.
23	Romantic for JACK and JILL.
24	Colourful (sunset?) for TRIO.
25	Snap B.O.
26	PALACE OF GOLD – SONG.
27	Acting Light.
28	Very. "Come Dancing" (Mirror Ball?) for TANGO.
29	Return to the state of LXQ.27.
30	Very dramatic – for PRISCILLA'S departure.
31	Even more dramatic – final moment before:
32	Fade B.O.
33	The Edge of the Forest (*Front Cloth*) – a very nice day.
34	Storm and Lightning.
35	Very mysterious – on the way to the Grotto.
36	Brighten as MOTHER GOOSE enters.
37	Very colourful (pulsing/ chasers?) for STRIP routine.
38	State of LXQ.36.
39	GROTTO seen through Gauze.
40	Gauze flie out – full GROTTO.

41   Very dramatic.
42   Dramatic for FINALE.
43   Fade F.O.H. with TABS.

                              ACT TWO
44   MEPHISTO DL.
45   FAIRY DR.
46   Lose MEPHISTO light DL.
47   VILLAGE GREEN seen through the Gauze.
48   Gauze flies out – VILLAGE GREEN – Lovely day – OPENING
         NUMBER.
49   As LXQ.48 but reduce slightly for scene.
50   Mock romantic for "THE HONEYSUCKLE AND THE BEE".
51   State of LXQ49.
52   Heroic for "WE'RE ON THE ROAD".
53   Snap B.O.
54   FAIRY DR.
55   Frontcloth (*Forest Gauze*) – bright for novelty marching routine
56   Snap B.O.
57   The Forest (*seen through the Front Gauze*) – Very dramatic and
         sinister – Night.
58   Gauze flies out – full stage – moonlight.
59   Snap B.O.
60   The Edge of the Forest (*Front Gauze*) – Moonlight.
61   Brighten slightly.
62   Romantic for duet.
63   Return to state of LXQ.61.
64   The clearing – very dramatic and sinister.
65   Transformation Lighting (cloud fx?).
66   Very romantic for Gooselake Ballet.
67   King Gander's Palace – still romantic but brighter.
68   Snap to very dramatic – harsh white light on MOTHER GOOSE for
         trial.
69   Return to state of LXQ.67.
70   Very bright for song and dance.
71   Sinister for MEPHISTO and fight.
72   Return to state of LXQ.70.
73   Snap B.O.
74   Front cloth – SONGSHEET.
75   Crossfade to very bright full stage for Walkdown and Finale.
76   Fade F.O.H. with Tabs – end of show.

Follow Spot Plot

ACT ONE

Cue	Effect – Stage R Follow	Effect – Stage L Follow
1	MEPHISTO DL.	
2		FAIRY DR.
1A	Snap B.O.	
2A		Fade B.O.
3	JACK C	JACK C.
3A	Letterbox for Chorus.	Letterbox for Chorus.
3B	X to JILL UL	X to JILL UL.
3C	Letterbox for Chorus.	Letterbox for Chorus.
3D	Fade B.O.	Fade B.O.
4	JACK C.	JILL C.
4A	Fade B.O.	Fade B.O.
5	MOTHER GOOSE C.	MOTHER GOOSE C.
5A	Fade B.O.	Fade B.O.
6	MEPHISTO DL.	
7		FAIRY DR.
6A	Snap B.O.	
7A		Snap B.O.
8	PRISCILLA DR follow to include JACK.	PRISCILLA DR to include JILL.
8A	Snap B.O.	Snap B.O.
9	MOTHER GOOSE C.	MOTHER GOOSE C.
9A	Colour wheel? for STRIP.	Colour wheel? for STRIP.
9B	Stabilise.	Stabilise.
9C	Fade B.O.	Fade B.O.
10	MOTHER GOOSE C.	MOTHER GOOSE C.
10A	Fade B.O.	Fade B.O.

ACT TWO

11	MEPHISTO D.L. .	
12		FAIRY D.R.
11A	Snap B.O.	
12A		Fade B.O.
13	MEPHISTO C.	MOTHER GOOSE C.
13A	Fade B.O.	Fade B.O.
14	JACK C.	JACK C.

14A Snap B.O.   Snap B.O.
15   FAIRY DR.   FAIRY DR.
15A Fade B.O.   Fade B.O.
16   JACK C.   JILL C.
16A Fade B.O.   Fade B.O.
17   MOTHER GOOSE C.   PRISCILLA C.
17A Snap B.O.   Snap B.O.
18   Letterbox for PRINCIPALS.   Letterbox for PRINCIPALS.
18A Snap B.O.   Snap B.O.
19   BOTH Follow through Walkdown then Letterbox for Finale.

Sound Plot

ACT ONE

Cue	Detail
1	Clap of THUNDER.
2	Clap of THUNDER.
3	Rhythmic clanking and whirring of EGG MACHINE.
4	Clap of THUNDER.
5	Very pretty Summery BIRDS.
6	Very pretty Summery BIRDS.
7	POT: "WHAT IS YOUR DESIRE?"
8	POT: "PLEASE".
9	POT: "WHAT IS YOUR DESIRE?"
10	POT: "WHAT DO YOU WANT THE UMBRELLA FOR?"
11	POT: "WHAT IS YOUR DESIRE?"
12	POT: "WHAT IS YOUR DESIRE?"
13	POT: "WHAT IS YOUR DESIRE?"
14	POT: "WHAT IS YOUR DESIRE?"
15	Clap of THUNDER into ferocious HURRICANE.
16	Gurgling, trickling fall of WATER.

ACT TWO

17	Clap of THUNDER.
18	Clap of THUNDER.
19	OWL.
20	Clap of THUNDER.

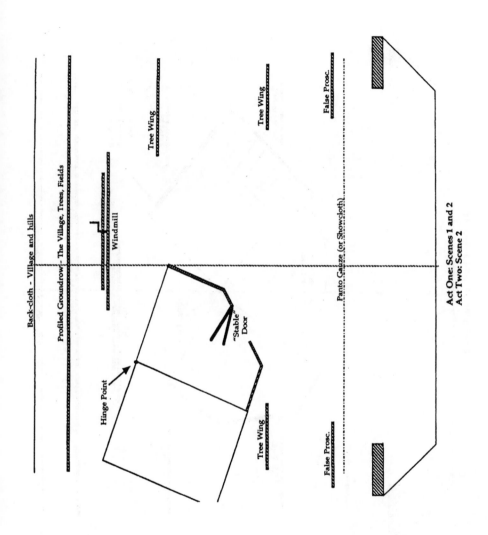

Back-cloth - Village and hills

Profiled Groundrow - The Village, Trees, Fields

Windmill

Tree Wing

Tree Wing

False Proc.

Panto Gauze (or Showcloth)

Hinge Point

"Stable" Door

Tree Wing

False Proc.

Act One: Scenes 1 and 2
Act Two: Scene 2

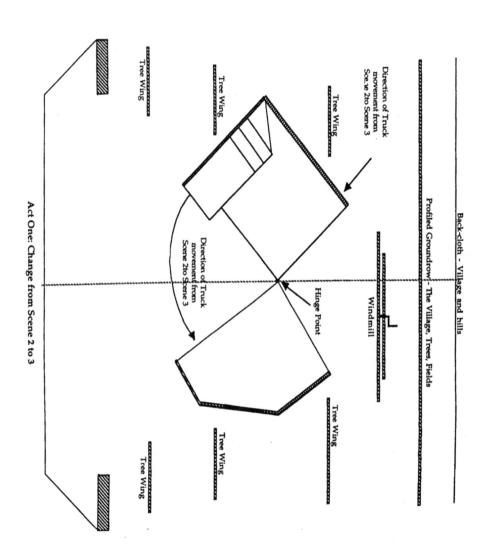

Back-cloth - Village and hills

Profiled Groundrow: The Village, Trees, Fields

Tree Wing

Direction of Truck movement from Scene 2 to Scene 3

Tree Wing

Tree Wing

Hinge Point

Windmill

Direction of Truck movement from Scene 2 to Scene 3

Tree Wing

Tree Wing

Tree Wing

Act One: Change from Scene 2 to 3

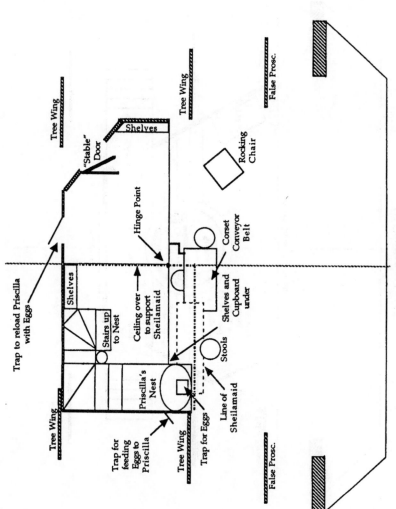

Tree Wing

Tree Wing

False Prosc.

"Stable" Door

Shelves

Rocking Chair

Hinge Point

Corset Conveyor Belt

Trap to reload Priscilla with Eggs

Shelves

Ceiling over to support Sheilamaid

Shelves and Cupboard under

Stairs up to Nest

Stools

Tree Wing

Priscilla's Nest

Line of Sheilamaid

Trap for feeding Eggs to Priscilla

Tree Wing

Trap for Eggs

False Prosc.

Act One: Scene 3

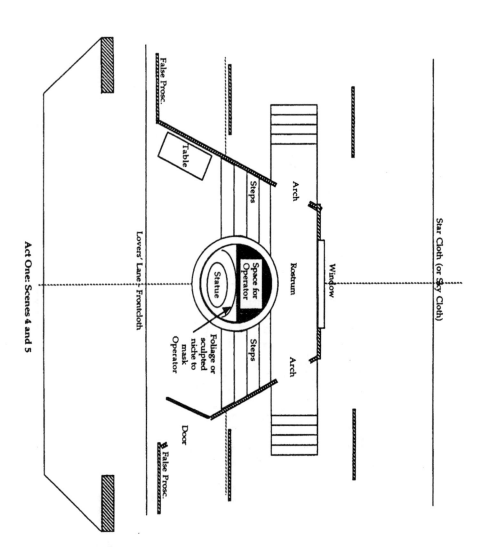

Act One: Scenes 4 and 5

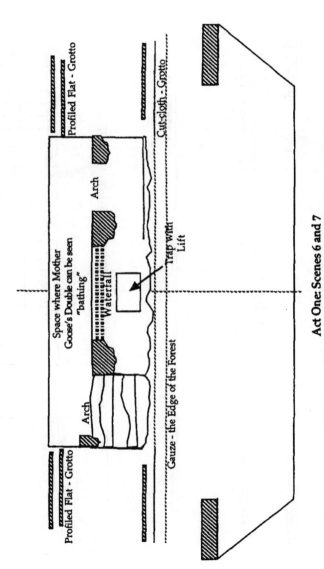

Space where Mother
Goose's Double can be seen
"bathing"

Profiled Flat - Grotto

Arch

Waterfall

Trap with
Lift

Cut-sloth - Grotto

Arch

Profiled Flat - Grotto

Gauze - the Edge of the Forest

Act One: Scenes 6 and 7
Edge of the Forest Gauze also for Act Two: Scenes 3 and 5

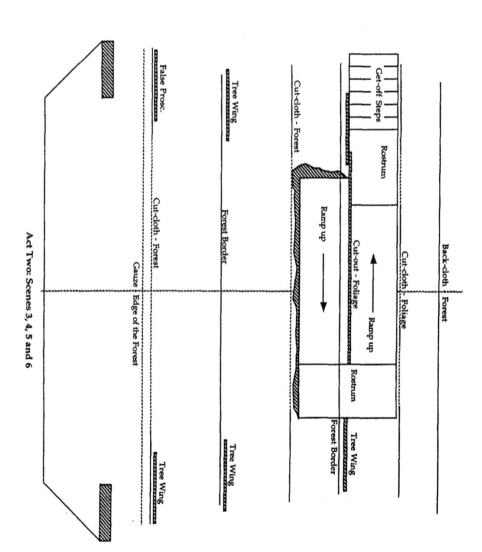

Act Two: Scenes 3, 4, 5 and 6

Back Cloth - King Gander's Palace

King Gander's Throne on Dais (truck)

Tree Wing

Cut-cloth - King Gander's Palace

Tree Wing

False Prosc.

Cut-cloth - King Gander's Palace

False Prosc.

Act Two: Scene 7